SUMMER OF THE MONSTERS

DAVID SODERGREN

For my mum and dad.
Thanks for all the holidays!

In the woods, darkness.
Ageless trees stand sentinel, as
gnarled roots stab violently into earth.
Branches intertwine like lovers' fingers,
sap bleeding betwixt fractured skin.
Strange. Silent.

In the woods, they slumber.
Eldritch. Unknowable.
A flash of light, spurting crimson.
And the screams.
Oh god, the screams.

In the woods, movement.
Scurrying limbs, dew drops
sparkling in frightened eyes.
Faster, and faster, and then?
Nothing.
The trees have seen it all.

In the woods, they rise.
Forgotten, yearning to rule again.
Older than the trees. Older than anything.
Wind whispers, caresses, halts as they pass.
Even the wind is afraid.
It should be.

For in the woods, they hunt.
And in the woods, they kill.

"Helsbridge"
Rupert Breckinmyer (18th Century)

Click-clack, clickety-clack,
Through the woods they come.
Click-clack, hide your crack,
They bite you on your bum.

Helsbridge playground rhyme
Author unknown

PART I

1

Dearest Lucy,
I'm dying.

LUCY BRANNIGAN CLUTCHED THE NOTE IN TREMBLING HANDS as the torn envelope fluttered lazily to the carpet.

I don't have long left.

The words stole her breath away.

She knew she would never make it to the chair, so she slumped to the floor, unsure what else to do. There were no clear protocols for situations like this; how to react to a parent's impending death was not taught in school, and certainly not by the parents themselves. Why would they? That would mean acknowledging the reality of the inevitable.

We are born, we live, and then we die.

When she tried to stand — to head to the kitchen and pour herself a glass of water — her unsteady legs refused to lift her. And so there Lucy remained, confused and disorientated on her living room floor, reading and re-reading the short note. The barely legible handwriting bore little resemblance to her father's once-impeccable cursive. A tear fell, dotting the page, the ink soaking through lined paper torn from one of his notepads. She was pleased to see he still used them.

Growing up, she remembered how all he cared about when buying new trousers was whether his notepad would slide comfortably into the pocket. If not, then no sale today, my friend.

Was he still like that? They hadn't spoken in such a long time. She would have to see him.

Before the end.

God, she didn't think she'd ever go home.

Home?

Could she still call it that? So many years had passed since she last walked Edinburgh's cobbled streets that the word 'home' felt fraudulent on her lips. Yet despite the passage of time, the people and places were indelibly etched in her mind. She had been born there, in Edinburgh's Royal Infirmary, in April 1980, and her mother had died there, in the same hospital, two days before Lucy's fourteenth birthday.

That was when the rot had set in.

Life had never been the same since her mother's death. Not for Lucy, and not for her father. She wasn't sure either of them had ever been happy again, although for a brief period during that summer... that special summer, the one with the monsters...

She folded the note and thought about the summer of 1996, those halcyon days when her favourite film was *The*

Crow, and Pearl Jam and the Smashing Pumpkins were on constant rotation on her Walkman.

Lying on the carpet, she fumbled her phone from her pocket and opened Spotify. She selected *1979* by the Smashing Pumpkins, and the music — as music is prone to doing — immediately transported her to those young and supposedly carefree days of teenage ennui and rebellion. Tears formed in her eyes, and she smiled as she remembered her father driving them halfway up the country in that awful white van. The skies had been leaden on that dismal day, the clouds fat and thunderous, and though it was twenty-eight years ago, Lucy still recalled *1979* playing when she glanced in the rearview mirror and saw — for the last time — Edinburgh receding into the distance.

Shit, she thought, as tears flowed down her cheeks. *It still feels like yesterday.*

2

———

June 1996

THE HEAVENS OPENED, THE SUDDEN DELUGE OF RAIN GIVING the van's feeble windscreen wipers their first test. Raindrops battered the roof, and Lucy adjusted her headphones and nudged the volume dial on her Walkman higher.

Edinburgh was a distant memory, though she harboured a secret fantasy that at some point during the journey, her dad would come to his senses, turn the van around, and drive them home. Their *real* home, the one that sold for considerably less than its valuation, a fact she had only learned from overhearing her dad talking to his agent on the phone.

Overhearing?

Okay, she had been snooping. But this wasn't just her father deciding what was for tea, or what colour to paint the bathroom walls.

Her entire *life* was at stake.

Two weeks' notice was all he had given her. The house had sold, and now they were moving north to a place she had never even heard of. She had no say in the matter, yet somehow her dad expected her to be happy — no, *enthusiastic* — about the situation.

What the hell did either of them know about the countryside? They were city dwellers, born and bred. The closest they ever came to the country was when her mum forced them to take day trips to Peebles or North Berwick. Those places were only a forty-minute drive from Edinburgh, and although to Lucy they felt as rural and isolated as a South American rainforest, this place — this town called Helsbridge — was three *hours* away.

She may as well be living on the moon.

Her dad was speaking to her, so she made a show of removing her headphones and letting them hang around her neck.

"What did you say?" she asked.

"I said, isn't it pretty?"

She saw him smiling to himself, and rolled her eyes.

Trees towered over them on either side as her dad navigated the wet and winding roads of the Scottish Highlands through endless miles of damp pine forests and neglected hiking trails, the sun a distant memory behind a thick ceiling of stormy grey clouds. With each turn, their worldly belongings slid from side-to-side in the back of the van. Everything they owned was packed in there, with plenty of space remaining. Any item her dad deemed unnecessary had been sold, and what *hadn't* sold was simply left behind.

"It's inspiring," he continued. "A new beginning."

"For you," she said. "This is the end for me."

"Nonsense. Wind down your window and smell that country air. Go on, do it!"

With a harumph, she forced the handle of the old van to

turn, lowering the window far enough to allow the rushing air to whistle through the gap.

"Mmmmm, isn't it wonderful?" her dad asked. "Breathe it in!"

Rain spattered her face. "It smells like wet dog."

He wasn't listening. "Aye, the countryside sure is something, eh?"

"It is," she said. "It is certainly something, *Brian.*"

Lucy took a perverse glee in calling her dad by his first name. Not only did it show how grown-up she was, but, more importantly, it also pissed him off. Normally, it was a win-win situation. Today, though, there was no souring his buoyant mood. She wound her window up and leaned her head against the seat. The day couldn't get any worse.

"Pass me my sunnies, would ya?" her dad asked, squinting at the hints of sun that glinted in broken fragments off the rain-slicked tarmac. She handed him his sunglasses, and he pulled a handkerchief from his pocket to wipe the lenses.

"Keep your eyes on the road," she said.

He ignored her and moved onto the second lens.

"Who even carries a hankie these days?"

"Lots of people." He turned to her. "They're very handy. If I ever need a bandage, or to carry—"

"Dad, watch out!"

The van bumped as they left the road, heading straight for a tree. Her dad spun the wheel, swerving onto the tarmac. For one second, two wheels left the ground, hovering above a ditch, before slamming back onto the road. Behind them, glass shattered as something heavy hit the floor of the van.

Lucy's hands tightened into fists.

"That better not be the TV."

Her dad waited too long before responding. "Ach, who needs a TV with a view like this?" he said, gesturing through the rain-streaked window at the looming mountains.

"Normal people."

"Normal is overrated," he countered, and Lucy placed her headphones back over her ears, irritated by his victory in their verbal sparring match. Normal *was* overrated, she couldn't argue with that. But come on, they needed a TV. What use was a video recorder without one? Ah, she knew what her dad would say.

The greatest television takes place in the human mind.

But he was an author, so of course he said dumb shite like that. It was what people used to pay him for. Yet, as the wipers worked frantically to clear the drizzle from the window, revealing strobing flashes of mist-wreathed mountains, Lucy had to admit that the scenery was definitely different to that of Edinburgh. Not *better*... but different. She cranked the volume on her Walkman as high as it would go and watched the trees blur by.

No television.

Jesus Christ, how was she expected to survive in the arse-end of nowhere without a TV? She could handle being taken away from her friends, because she didn't have any, and though she'd miss the record stores, she no longer had any money to buy things. But no TV? That was practically child abuse.

"Lucy!"

Wearily, she lowered her headphones again. "What now?"

"We're approaching Helsbridge." He nodded to himself. "Our nearest town."

Our nearest town.

The words sent shivers down Lucy's spine. Not *our* town,

but our *nearest* town. How far from civilisation *were* they? Visions of decrepit mountain shacks shimmered through her mind, the pair of them bedding down for the night in sleeping bags beneath a ragged gazebo canopy.

"Here we go!" her dad said, and drummed a beat on the steering wheel. "Look out, Helsbridge, the Brannigans are here!"

The sign for the town was hidden amongst ferns and bushes. They shot past it, carrying on until Helsbridge revealed itself in all its sad glory.

"Oh god," Lucy muttered.

It was so small.

Helsbridge was a glorified main street, lined on one side with tacky shops, a Post Office, and a cafe. And on the other? A few scattered houses and a shop selling pottery, the once-white paintwork a dull slate colour in the miserable weather.

"Where is everything?" she asked. "Where's the school?"

"Your new school is in Kingussie. That's the next town over."

"How do I get there? You're not taking me in this death trap."

"There's a school bus. It'll be perfect. You can make friends before the end of term, and then you'll have someone to play with over the summer."

Someone to play with.

Jeez, did he think she was five years old? She was *sixteen*.

The thought depressed her. Sixteen years old, and already her life was finished. She stared out the window at an old church that looked like it hadn't held a service for decades. Branches slithered through broken windows, and a tree had burst through the roof. She peered at it, and then the decrepit building, and the town she had no choice but to call home, were behind her.

The van slowed to a standstill beside a tall, stone monument. Her dad pulled a crumpled map from under his seat, and Lucy waited, gazing at the brass plaque affixed to the cenotaph.

FOR THOSE WHO LOST THEIR LIVES IN BATTLE, the sign read, followed by a list of illegible names.

"Not far now," her dad said, the exhaust belching smoke as he started the van and took a left turn. "So, what did you think of our new home town?"

"Where's the rest of it?"

"What else do you need? You've got nature on your doorstep, Lucy. Some people would kill for that."

"In the fifties, sure. I don't know if you've been keeping up, *Brian*, but it's nineteen-ninety-*six*. We have cinemas and bowling alleys and record shops now."

"We had all of those in the fifties."

"Yeah, you'd know," she grumbled. Why did he always have an answer for everything? "Okay, what about arcades?" He started to reply, and she cut him off. "And I don't mean pinball machines, smart guy. I mean *proper* arcades. Did they have those?"

"Nope. Guess you'll have to go without *Pac-Man* for a while." He put his hand on her knee, and said, in the most sarcastic voice Lucy had ever heard, "However will you *manage?*"

"Ugh, you're such a loser." She moved her leg out of reach and glared at the electricity pylons cutting across rolling fields dotted with farmhouses. On her dad's side was a forest so thick it looked impenetrable.

"They're Scots Pine," he said.

"Huh?"

"The trees you're looking at. They're Scots Pine. I read it in the brochure."

"Whatever," she shrugged.

They took a right turn onto a dirt track and entered the forest. Inside, the light vanished, plunging them into darkness. Her dad switched the headlights on as the vehicle bumped and shuddered over potholes that rattled the frame and shook the broken glass in the rear.

Please don't be the TV, she thought. But what else could it be? It's not like they'd packed a collection of priceless crystal vases.

The van ploughed on through the forest. Branches scraped across the windows as if trying to gain entry, and Lucy shrank into her seat. She didn't like it here. At least back home, she could tell when some drunk was going to harass her for spare change, or when a group of laddies were up to mischief, or when a car was about to run the red light. But here? In the woods? You could touch the wrong plant and die, or get bitten by a snake and die, or get lost and, well... die.

It was no way to live.

"Almost there," her dad said. "According to the map, it should be just around the corner."

"I can't believe you've never been here."

"I've seen photos of the inside. It looks nice. Bigger than our old place."

"*Recent* photos?"

"Don't worry, it's not been condemned." He grinned at her. "As far as I know."

The van turned sharply, the canopy of trees thinning. A clearing opened up before them, revealing a vast field backed by more woodland, with a two-storey stone farmhouse gleaming like a beacon in the centre.

Lucy screwed up her eyes. Was she seeing things? The building was surrounded by—

Her dad slammed on the brakes, jolting them into their seatbelts.

She guessed he'd noticed them too.

Whick, whick, went the windscreen wipers.

Her dad leaned forwards, muttering, "What the hell...?"

Whick, whick.

The rain continued to fall.

"Dad," Lucy said quietly, as the wipers jolted back and forth, smearing the water across the glass. "Who the fuck are all those people?"

3

———

HER DAD DIDN'T ANSWER, AND WHEN LUCY TURNED TO HIM, he wore an expression of total confusion.

He was not being helpful, so she looked back at the bizarre assemblage of people spread out across the clearing. "Are you sure this is the place?"

"Yeah," he mumbled. "Maybe it's... a welcoming party?"

He put the van in gear and edged into the clearing. At least twenty men and women in a variety of outfits loitered around the building, one perched atop a bicycle, another dressed as an old-fashioned policeman. Two more sat on a horse-drawn carriage, while a butcher stood with his fist raised in protest at a motionless pug dog with a string of sausages ensnared in its mouth.

Motionless...

"Shit," said Lucy. "They're not real."

The closer they came, the more the artifice revealed itself. The people were mannequins, frozen in time like panels from a comic strip. They drove past a clown, the propellor on his too-small hat spinning idly in the breeze.

"Scarecrows," her dad said, and chuckled hollowly. "Cool, huh?" He didn't sound like he meant it.

Lucy stared at the blank faces of a lifeless bride and groom, and before she had a chance to ponder what the mannequins were supposed to be scaring off, the van came to a stop.

"Well," her dad said. "What do you think?"

"You mean, apart from," — she gestured around them — "the haunted field?"

"Yeah." He shook his head. "The brochure never mentioned *that.*"

She wasn't sure what to say. The house looked — from the outside, at least — to be in pretty good nick. Her dad had told her the previous family left in a hurry, and that their furniture and appliances were included in the sale... but she couldn't always trust him. Over the past two years, he had told too many lies about the state of their finances. Like most parents, he seemed to have fooled himself into thinking his daughter couldn't tell when he was lying, forgetting that after the Santa Claus debacle, children treated every utterance from their parents with supreme suspicion.

"So?" her dad asked.

She inspected the building. White walls, a red door, lots of windows and lots of rooms. Far bigger than their expensive flat back in Edinburgh.

"Can we afford this?"

"Ha!" he said, laughing too loudly. "Of course we can, my ever-questioning offspring. No problemo."

Lucy gave him her most adult stare, the one she had learned from her mum. "Dad, seriously..."

He scratched his chin and looked away. "We can afford it. With the money from our old place, and the stuff we sold... we'll be okay. We'll be fine." He opened the door and got out. "And anyway, it was real cheap."

He stood in the rain waiting for her, but she wasn't ready yet. *This* was the place they were going to call home for the foreseeable future. This farmhouse in the middle of a clearing, surrounded by a battalion of scarecrows and miles of thick woodland. What the fuck was she going to do here? She wasn't a kid anymore. Did her dad expect her to kill an entire summer exploring a forest? She was an *adult,* dammit. No *way* could she live here. She would stagnate, emerging in twenty years as a bitter old crone who had spoken to no one but her father and her field of ghoulish scarecrows for two decades.

Her dad tapped on her window, and she jumped.

"Shall we take a look inside?" he asked, his voice muffled by the glass.

"Fine," she said, opening the door and getting out. "But only because the van stinks of your farts."

"My darling daughter, ladies and gentlemen."

She muttered, "You're so lame," and stood beside him in the rain. The sky was dark, the trees oppressive, and other than the hum of the wind and an occasional bird call, all was silent.

It made Lucy uneasy. Already, she missed the roar of cars and the chatter of people, the noise of construction workers and the shrill *beep beep* of traffic lights. This quietness was unnatural.

Her dad placed a hand on her shoulder. "All this is ours."

"Yup," she said, unable to muster up any zeal.

"Did you see our barn on the drive in?"

"Huh?"

"Our barn. Come on, I'll show you."

With the untrimmed lawn soaking their trainers and

trousers, he led her around the house, past fuel canisters and metal buckets and a broken ladder.

"Look," her dad said.

Lucy followed his pointing finger towards a large wooden shed that sat before the wall of trees.

"We've got our own barn," he said. "Isn't that neat?"

"Terrific," she grumbled. "We can keep *all* our horses there."

The sarcasm was not lost on him, but he carried on regardless. "I might turn it into a workspace. My own private office, once I've got things going again."

"And when's that gonna be? How long are we staying here? You said it wouldn't be forever. You promised me."

"It won't be, Luce."

She hated when he called her Luce, almost as much as he hated when she called him Brian.

"Like I said," he continued, "we'll be here until we've got money coming in again. When the new book is done, and I've turned things—"

"A new book? You've started writing again?"

"I mean, not *started*, per se, but I've got some ideas. Some *great* ideas. It'll be different now, honestly. Living here, free from distractions. I'll be able to just sit and write." He smiled wistfully. "Like the old days."

Free from distractions.

She knew what he meant. Free from *memories*. The ghost of her mother haunted every nook of their old home. Sometimes, Lucy thought she heard her mum calling her down for tea, or smelt her perfume lingering in the air. Now even that small comfort was gone. Resentment simmered within her. But towards who? Her dad for bringing her here? Yes, but also towards her mum for leaving her. It was ridiculous to feel that way — her mum hadn't walked in front of that truck deliberately — but she couldn't help it.

"Okay," her dad said. "The barn can wait. Let's go inside."

He marched through the grass and Lucy trailed after him, her Pearl Jam hoodie drenched from the rain, the wet sleeves hanging beyond her fingertips. As she walked, she glanced at the grim forest that surrounded her, so tall and overwhelming, and at the nightmarish tableaux of figures in the front yard.

She started to cry.

She hated it here.

And more than anything... she didn't belong.

4

———

Hᴇʀ ᴅᴀᴅ ᴡᴀs ᴡᴀɪᴛɪɴɢ ʙʏ ᴛʜᴇ ғʀᴏɴᴛ ᴅᴏᴏʀ ᴡɪᴛʜ ᴀ ᴋᴇʏ ɪɴ ʜɪs hand.

"Door wasn't even locked," he said. "Can you believe that? It's so safe here, we don't need to. Bet you wouldn't find anyone who does *that* in Edinburgh!"

"It's because there's no one around."

"Well, I think it's reassuring. And anyway, Helsbridge is only two miles away." He pushed the door open and entered, muttering, "We're hardly stranded on a desert island."

Lucy stayed back in case the unlocked door was a sign the Manson family had moved in, but when she peered out from behind her father, she saw a hallway lined with photos and paintings, and a grandfather clock at the far end. Shoes were piled up along the wall, and tweed jackets and colourful raincoats hung from brass hooks.

"Umm, are you *sure* we're in the right place?" asked Lucy.

"Aye. Told you the previous family moved out in a hurry."

"And left their jackets and shoes?"

"Some sort of emergency, the estate agent told me."

"What kind?"

"I didn't ask."

"The inquisitive mind of the author," she said. "Fuck's sake, dad."

He ignored her. Ever since Lucy's mum's passing, her dad had stopped chastising her for her language, and allowed her to do things she never would have gotten away with under her mum's watchful eye. Renting eighteen-rated movies, staying out late, even getting her eyebrow pierced... nothing was off-limits these days. She figured if she started smoking crack cocaine, he'd nod and mumble, *"It's good for teenagers to have hobbies."*

He opened the nearest door, and Lucy followed him into the living room. It was as if they had walked into a family home while the occupants were on holiday. There were chairs, a settee, side tables, shelving units, and cabinets full of books and board games. Dying potted plants lined the windowsills, and on the wall hung an ugly painting of a smiling family, the crude oil work rendering their faces smeary, indistinct blotches. It had everything, except...

"There's no TV in here," said Lucy.

"We have a TV."

"I mean one that isn't broken."

"We don't know it's broken," he said, and left the room. Feeling like Goldilocks, Lucy took a last look around and scurried after her father. She found him in the kitchen, flicking the kettle on and off and grinning at dirty dishes stacked on the worktop.

"I can't believe it," he said. "All this is ours."

"Don't you think it's a bit weird?"

"Weird? I guess so, but I'm not complaining. Look, we've got a microwave again!"

That *was* an exciting development. It had been six months since their old one had packed in. But Lucy couldn't shake the feeling her dad knew more than he was letting on.

"So you're telling me the family who lived here just left one day, taking nothing with them?"

Her dad opened the washing machine and gazed inside like he expected to see a majestic vista. "Sure seems that way."

"Uh-huh. And you don't find that suspicious?"

"As a family who just moved house," he said patronisingly, "no, I don't find a family moving house to be suspicious. Shit, I don't even find it interesting. Look at all this stuff. We don't need to buy anything!"

"Except for a TV."

"Who needs one? You've got nature's TV out every window!"

"I don't *want* nature's TV, Brian, because last time I checked, they weren't showing *The X-Files*. And what about my videos? I want to watch *The Crow* and—"

"Well, you can't!" he said through gritted teeth. *"Okay?* If we don't have a television, you're going to have to wait, because we damn well can't afford one."

"That's not fair," said Lucy, "How do you expect me to—"

"I don't expect *anything* from you other than bitching and moaning," he snapped. "We're broke, Lucy. We're flat broke, okay?"

"But you said—"

"I know what I said, and I'm sorry. But this place... this house is the first bit of genuine luck we've had in months."

Tears welled in her eyes. "What about the money from our house?"

"Most of what was left over went on overdue bills, and the rest is all we've got to live on until I've got cash coming in again, and I don't know when that'll be. My publisher folded, and no one wants my old books, and I can't... I mean, I keep trying to write a new one, but ever since..." He took a deep breath, and turned to look out the window. She thought he was crying. "Ever since your mum died, I can't make it work. I keep trying, but *nothing works.*"

"I could get a job." She forced a smile. "You know I hate school."

"No. An education is important. You've lost everything else. I'm not going to let you lose that too."

Shit. That only made her cry harder. She hated when he said sweet things, and shuffled closer, putting her arms around him. "I've not lost *everything,*" she said, her cheeks burning in embarrassment.

He placed his hands on her shoulders and moved her back, staring at her face. She knew he was about to say something cheesy.

"Dad, don't you dare—"

"I love you, Lucy."

"Oh god," she laughed, wiping away her tears. "This is so lame."

"I know." He cleared his throat and released her. "Look, neither of us like this. But we have to try to make it work, okay? It's just the two of us now, and honestly, I have no idea what I'm doing."

"I know. It took you six months to notice my eyebrow piercing."

"It's very subtle."

"Sure, dad. Now, as much as I'd love to spend all summer crying in the kitchen with you, why don't you show me my room so I can get unpacked?"

He smiled. Not the village idiot smile he used when he pretended everything was fine and dandy, but his real smile, broad and warm. "I thought I'd let you choose."

"That's the least you could do after dragging me halfway across the country."

"Go on then," he said. "There are three rooms upstairs, and I bet I can guess which one you'll pick."

"We'll see!" she called, and ran from the kitchen to the stairs, her feet pounding the wooden steps. God, that was so awkward. She and her dad, weeping in front of each other. She knew things were bad, but not *that* bad. How oblivious and self-involved was she? He was trying to keep a roof over their heads, and all she did was whinge about not having a TV. What was she, a teenager? She laughed at that, and reached the top of the stairs.

Three doors awaited her.

Behind the first was a boringly normal adult bedroom. She gazed at the pale blue walls, and the elegant cream and gold bed sheets. Her posters would hide most of the bland colour, and with the addition of her leopard print duvet cover and some fairy lights, it could feel like home. And what was behind that door in the corner? A walk-in closet? That would be awesome.

She opened the door and stepped inside an en-suite bathroom.

"Holy shit."

A shower, a sink, and a toilet all to herself? Her grinning reflection stared back at her from the cabinet mirror, and she could contain herself no longer.

"Oh my *god!*" she yelled, sticking her tongue out at her reflection before running and flopping onto the bed, not caring that her soggy hoodie soaked the duvet and its ugly sheets.

"Told you I could guess," her dad shouted from downstairs, as she kicked her feet on her new bed in a delightfully childish manner. Even fully grown sixteen-year-old adults need to cut loose now and again, she reasoned. Still, she hadn't checked the other rooms. Maybe her dad was tricking her? She got up, leaving a Lucy-shaped damp mark on the sheets, and investigated the next room. It was cramped and boxy and full of junk, and she had to stand on her tiptoes to see out of the one small window.

"Fuck that," she said. This could be her dad's office until he cleared out the barn, which she figured would happen sometime around the tenth of Never.

The last room was a decent size, but it had no private bathroom, and the closets — whilst spacious — were sliding doors covered from floor to ceiling in mirrors. The idea appalled her. Who the hell wants to see themselves sitting on the bed in their underwear clipping their toenails?

"Easiest choice I've ever made," she said, as she walked to the window and stared out at the forest. From this high vantage point, she got an idea of its vastness. The trees stretched as far as she could see, all the way to the distant, snow-capped peaks of the mountains. Her mum would have loved this view. Of the three of them, it was she who had adored the countryside, and who often wiled away the hours wandering amongst flowers and trees while Lucy and her dad stayed home.

And now, gazing out over the flowing green landscape, Lucy began to understand why.

She felt insignificant before it. The scale of the forest, and the unknowable age of the trees — Scots Pine, her dad had said — filled her with an unfamiliar sense of awe. A shiver sparkled down her spine and raised gooseflesh on her arms. The sensation embarrassed her, and when she started to cry, all she could do was stare out at the trees in bewilderment. God, she missed her mum. This might have been bearable with her along for the ride.

Something moved along the edge of the forest, catching her eye. A large, dark shape slipped into the trees, then disappeared. A bear? Did bears live in the Highlands? No, of course not.

"Just tired," she said, and forced a laugh, which only brought more tears. She stared out the window, and whispered, "I wish you could have seen this."

"Lucy? You up there?"

"Shit." She wiped her eyes on her sleeve as her dad's ponderous footsteps thudded on the stairs. "Yeah, I'm in here." Arming herself with her most aloof expression, she met him on the landing. He carried two bags of clothes and a hiking rucksack she doubted had ever been used.

"Van's open if you want to unpack," he said, muscling his way past her into the bedroom.

"Where do you think you're going?"

He turned to her blankly. "You... you want the en-suite room, right?"

"No," she said, surprising herself. She looked out the window. "This is my room."

"You sure? Because the main bathroom is downstairs, and—"

"I don't care. I want this one."

"Really?"

"Jeez, are you having a stroke? This is my room, so get out." She ushered him onto the landing. "No dads allowed."

"So let me get this straight. The en-suite is mine?"

"You need it. Can't have you going to the bathroom in

the night and falling down the stairs. You'll break a hip, and men your age need to be careful."

"I don't understand you at all," he said with a wry grin.

"That's part of my charm."

He started down the corridor, then sheepishly turned. "Uh, one thing. The TV... I'm afraid it didn't make it."

"That's okay," said Lucy, gesturing towards her window. "I have nature's TV right here." She smiled at him, and his face creased. She knew what was coming next. "Don't cry, Brian. And whatever you're thinking of saying, do *not* say it. If you tell me you love me again, I'm throwing myself out of the window, understand?"

"Gotcha," he said, giving her a thumbs up like the lamewad he was.

Lucy closed the door on him and took in the sights of her new room. With a few posters and—

The door opened, and her dad's head appeared, bearing his goofball grin. "I love you," he said, and then he was gone, skipping along the hallway.

"You're such a loser!" she called after him.

There was no way they were related. There must have been a mixup in the hospital. She looked around her room again, but found her gaze naturally drawn to the forest. *Had* she seen something out there? Like a really, *really* big dog? Possibly. Maybe she'd investigate the woods tomorrow and find out. After all, her mum had adored wandering through nature, so it couldn't be all bad. It was what *she* would have done.

She turned away, and caught a glimpse of herself in the mirrored sliding doors. Her black eyeliner ran down her cheeks, and her hair was a mess. She looked like she'd just staggered home from a night of drunken revelry.

"Well, those mirrors have to go," she said, and sprinted down the stairs to collect her meagre belongings from the van. She had a room to decorate, and the forest — and whatever lived in there — would just have to wait.

5

———————

Before she started unpacking, Lucy stripped the room bare. Everything that didn't belong to her — other than the furniture — had to go. Luckily, it appeared to be a guest room or something, so she didn't have to empty drawers of other people's knickers.

As instructed by her father, she turfed out anything that would fit through the window, where it would be dragged into a pile for a bonfire whenever it stopped raining. She was forced to keep the existing mattress and bedding, as they didn't have their own, but other than that, everything went. The first item she unpacked was her CD/cassette player, followed by the CD tower into which she slid her albums. She settled on The Smashing Pumpkins' *Siamese Dream* as her decorating music, and got to work. Soon, posters of Pearl Jam, The Wildhearts, and Alice in Chains covered the reflective cupboard doors, though she kept one free to use as a full-length mirror.

By eight o'clock, she was almost done, her clothes stuffed clumsily into a chest of drawers while she laboured over more important details, like alphabetising her videos and making a collage of photos. Her stomach growled angrily at her, and she realised she hadn't eaten since that lunchtime stop at the Little Chef on the drive up.

Downstairs, she found pasta and bolognese sauce in the kitchen, both of which were still in date, and made dinner before trudging upstairs to fetch her dad, who was pottering around in his office, unloading and arranging his writing equipment. Taking pride of place in the centre of his crookedly assembled desk — DIY had never been his forte — was something new.

"Is that a typewriter?"

"How did you know?" he replied in mock surprise.

"I only meant—"

"With keen observational skills like that, I sure hope you follow in your old man's footsteps as a writer. You—"

"Oh god, enough already! I don't know why I bother."

He laughed and tried to ruffle her hair, and she dodged out of his way. "I thought I'd get back to my roots," he said. "I wrote my first novel on this baby, and that didn't turn out so bad."

"You sold the word processor, didn't you?"

"That's right," he said, smiling at his typewriter like a lunatic. "Don't need it when I've got ol' Bertha here."

"But didn't mum buy you that for your—"

"Something smells good. Is tea ready?"

Lucy didn't answer. She *couldn't* answer. She looked at the photo frame on his desk, a picture of her mum taken in the seventies. In the photo, she wore red dungarees over a yellow bikini, and held an ice cream cone in each hand.

Her dad saw her looking. "I didn't want to sell it, believe me. But—"

"You want your dinner or not?" said Lucy. Her eyes tingled.

"Sure. I'll see you down there. Gimme two minutes."

When he eventually joined her at the dining table, they were both so tired they ate in silence. Her dad woke her at nine, which came as a shock to Lucy, as she was still sitting at the table on the hard wooden chair. Wiping the drool from her chin in shame, she said goodnight and made her way up the stairs while her father tidied up.

"We've got a dishwasher!" she heard him cry as she plodded into her room. A combination of the long drive, the country air, and all the unpacking and decorating had taken its toll, and she kicked off her jeans and hoodie and collapsed onto the bed in her t-shirt and undies. She worried she would have trouble falling asleep in a new house.

Seconds later, she was out for the count.

~

During the night, Lucy only awoke once, and that was because of the scream.

"The fuck was that?" she groaned, lying still and waiting for sleep to take her into its dreamy embrace once more. But when the scream came again, louder and more urgent, she sat up. The curtains were open, moonlight flooding in and bathing the room in a cool blue glow. Rain pattered off the windowpane, and she got out of bed and stumbled sleepily to the window.

To her horror, she caught a glimpse of herself in the mirror. One side of her hair was flat against her head, and her underpants had rolled below her belly. She tugged them up and snapped the elastic into place, then looked over her shoulder at the poster of Brandon Lee in *The Crow*.

"I'm sorry you had to see that," she said, and once more

heard the scream. This time, she was awake enough to recognise it as the terrified shriek of a girl. She opened the window and leaned out.

The freezing night air stung her bare arms.

"Is anyone there?" she half-shouted, mindful not to wake her dad.

No one replied.

She waited a while, shivering by the window and listening to the wind swaying the branches and rustling the pine needles, but the scream never came again.

It was probably kids fooling around. What else was there to do in a dead-end town like Helsbridge? Lucy wondered if one day she would be hanging out in the woods, making bad decisions and smoking illicit substances with her buddies.

Forming lasting friendships was never something she excelled at, but this was a new town. *A new beginning,* her dad had said. She no longer had to play the part of the girl everyone picked on. Here, in Helsbridge, she could be whoever she wanted to be. And with that cautiously optimistic thought playing in her mind, Lucy unpicked a serious wedgie and slipped back under the covers, cocooning herself in the soft cotton.

Anyone I want to be, she thought, and then she was asleep once more.

~

Click-clack, click-clack.

Fiona ran.

They were following, and they wanted to kill her, and it was all her own stupid fault. Her parents had warned her, but she hadn't listened, she hadn't *believed*. Why would she? What they had told her was absurd.

Impossible.

Monsters weren't real. Everybody knew that.

And yet...

Click-clack, click-clack.

They were gaining on her. She couldn't outrun them.

They had too many legs.

They've always been here, Fiona, her mother had said.

But lately, her father had added, *they've grown bolder.*

She had laughed. Goddammit, she had *laughed* at her parents and their dumb superstitions.

She wasn't laughing now.

Click-clack, click-clack, click-clack.

She held her hands up to protect herself from the branches that whipped across her skin. Warm blood trickled down her face and palms. She couldn't fall.

Falling would mean death.

"Please," she sobbed. "Leave me alone!"

Click-clack, click-clack, click-clack.

There. Through the trees.

A house.

Safety.

Sanctuary.

She increased her pace, her lungs close to bursting. Close, so close. Panic flowed through her veins; a blind, crazed panic that flooded her with adrenaline.

She wasn't far now.

Would they follow her into the clearing?

Her foot caught a root, and she stumbled, pinwheeling her arms to maintain balance. Against impossible odds, she kept her footing, slamming into a tree and carrying on. Five years of tennis coaching had finally paid off.

Click-clack, click-clack, click-clack.

She saw the house clearly. The old Chow residence.

Oh god, no.

Fiona had heard the rumours. The playground tales, whispered between children in hushed tones.

The monsters got them, they said. *They got them, and they ate them, and they were never seen again.*

Why hadn't she listened? Why hadn't she *believed?*

Click-clack, click-clack, click-clack, click-clack.

A few more steps and she would be in the clearing. Then, she could reach the house.

Just a few... more... steps...

The body hit like a runaway boulder, slamming into her with such force that she felt her spine snap. The impact brought her crashing onto a bed of pine needles, and though the damp ground softened the blow, it was the last bit of good fortune in the girl's miserably short life.

For the monsters descended on her, hacking at her limbs, her thin rain-jacket and knock-off Wranglers useless to protect her from the snapping claws that closed over her wrists and ankles, crushing her bones with fearsome power and grinding them to dust. They dragged her through the woods at high speed, and when they stopped, and Fiona looked up into the black, lifeless eyes that encircled her, the monsters attacked in a flesh-tearing frenzy. Serrated claws hacked into her belly, opening her up, her lifeblood fountaining from the wound and sparkling in the moonlight.

A claw dug into her thigh, slicing through the tender meat and crunching the bone as the monster wrenched her leg free, the ripping of denim and flesh indivisible in the girl's mind. More of the creatures emerged from the shadows, fighting over her severed leg, each battling to claim the trophy as their own.

She rolled onto her side, fingers digging into the soft earth as she tried to drag herself away, her guts spooling out of the cavity in her abdomen and slopping onto the forest floor. But the movement alerted them, and they pounced once more, tearing her apart with inhuman savagery.

And when the sun rose the next morning, casting golden rays across the forest and turning the sky red, all that remained of the girl — of the foolish girl who hadn't believed — were some shredded clothes and a mottled clump of dark, bloody hair.

For her, the fleeting dream of life had come to an end.

6

———

THE SUN WOKE LUCY LONG BEFORE SHE WANTED TO GET UP, so she rose early for a much-needed shower. After, over breakfast, she asked her dad if he had heard anything during the night.

"Nope," he said, shoving a spoonful of Cornflakes into his mouth. "Slept like a log. How about you? You wake up drooling like last night at the dinner table?"

"Five minutes." She gave him a slow clap. "You managed a full *five minutes* without bringing it up."

He chuckled and jabbed his spoon into the cereal.

"We should go food shopping," said Lucy, staring at her own half-full bowl. "I don't like eating someone else's stuff. It feels icky."

He nodded, and finished chewing before he spoke. "I agree. There's something a little macabre about this."

"Totally."

"On the other hand, it's kinda wasteful to throw out perfectly good food, and these people had expensive tastes. Have you seen their wine? Yowza!"

"I'm not old enough to drink," she replied. "So I wouldn't know."

"Oh, that's right. You've never touched a drop, have you?"

"Not once."

"So who is it that drinks half my wine and replaces it with water, thinking that I — a wine *connoisseur* — won't notice?"

"Connoisseur, huh? Is that a fancy man's way of saying he's an alcoholic?"

She waited for a retort, but instead, he looked at her askew. "You're in a suspiciously good mood this morning."

"I was until you pointed it out."

"Damn," he said, as he tidied the bowls from the table and gleefully stacked them in the dishwasher. "Mental note; never make an observation."

"So, are we going shopping? Maybe see the magical sights of Helsbridge?" She tilted her head at him. "I got that right, yeah? *Sights,* like, plural? Or is it only the war memorial?"

"Apparently there's a stone circle nearby, and a witch's grave in the next town over, but we should save some excitement for next week."

"Wow, at least now I've got something to look forward to."

"You start your new school tomorrow. Is that not thrilling enough?" Before she could answer, he said, "Let's do the shopping later, 'kay? I want to get to work."

"You starting a new book?"

A faraway look came over him, one she hadn't seen in a while. *His thinking face,* her mum used to call it. "I've got an idea, locked in here," — he tapped his temple — "and I just have to pry it free. It's good, though. I swear, Lucy... this book is gonna be the one to put me back on the map. There's something in the air here, don'tcha think?"

"If you say so."

"I do."

She got up from the table. "Well, if we're not getting groceries today, I'm gonna explore the forest."

"*You're* gonna—" He looked like he was about to make fun of her, then changed his mind. "Cool. Great idea."

"Yeah. Seeing as our TV is still lying in the van in a pile of broken glass, I figured I've nothing better to do."

"Okay. But don't get lost. Those woods go deep."

"Aye aye, captain," she said, and saluted him, before heading up the stairs to prepare for a day of adventuring.

Don't get lost?

She laughed at that.

God, her dad could be such a dork sometimes.

She dug her winter jacket out of the closet — sure, it was almost July, but this was Scotland — and stuffed a bottle of Irn Bru and a packet of crisps in her schoolbag, trying not to think of what fresh horrors Monday would bring. School wold break for summer on Friday, but her dad had insisted she go in for those last few days.

You have to ingratiate yourself, he had said. *Make some friends for the summer, unless you want to spend it with me.*

That was a fate she did not relish, especially with no TV. Her books and music could sustain her for a while, but not all summer. Some friends would be nice. Even *one* friend.

She slung her schoolbag over her shoulder and marched out of the house. A cool breeze blew, but the rain had stopped, and the sun kept threatening to appear from behind the clouds.

The scarecrows seemed less spooky today. She inspected them as she passed, thinking about the awesome photographs she could take, if only her dad hadn't sold her camera. She decided her favourite pair were the male and female mannequins that lay on the grass in matching striped swimwear and sunglasses. Them, or the lumberjack with the axe raised high above his head. Something about his powerful stance and rugged, bearded face sent confusing messages through her brain.

Before heading into the forest, Lucy investigated the barn. It reminded her of the one from that horrible film her dad had rented a few years ago, *Arachnophobia,* and the prospect of coming face-to-face with a shed full of rampaging spiders sent chills through her. On closer inspection, it was just a big ol' barn, with a large generator in the front and five empty horse stalls. A pitchfork, an axe, and a rusted scythe hung from hooks on the wall, while a rickety ladder led to an upper level. She prodded the wooden rungs, and decided she didn't trust them. Better to let her dad try it out first, preferably with an ambulance on standby.

She left the barn and wandered to the edge of the forest, pacing the perimeter until she located a path. Well, not so much a *path* as a trail of trampled vegetation, but it would suffice.

"Goodbye, cruel world," she said with a smile, and followed the trail into the forest. It had to lead somewhere. Trails didn't end. They took people places, or circled back on themselves. Otherwise, what was the point of them?

Fallen pine needles, turned to mulch by the rain, coated the ground, so Lucy hopped from stone to grassy clod in an effort to not muddy her trainers. They were her last remaining pair of shoes, and she needed them for school tomorrow. If she showed up in filthy trainers, she'd be labelled a scaff and *never* make any friends.

As she walked, she wondered how differently things would have worked out if her mum hadn't died. Would they still be living in Edinburgh? She thought so. God, had it really been two years since her death? She still remembered the funeral with unnerving accuracy, her dad gripping her hand and trying to remain stoic as *Unchained Melody* played, before breaking down during the climactic crescendo.

Would he marry again?

No one could ever replace her mum, but her dad deserved a little happiness, and it would be nice for him to have someone other than his daughter to bother with his nonsense.

The trail kept going, leading deeper into the woods. The previous night's rainwater dripped from spindly branches, landing on her head and occasionally trickling down the back of her neck. Birds chirruped all around, and she picked up a pine cone and threw it at a tree. The sound it made when striking the bark was immensely satisfying, and she tried again. The noise of the city was a million miles away, and it felt good.

Amazing, actually.

She thought she'd miss it, and maybe in time she would, but right now, alone in a forest surrounded by nothing but the squawks and drips and rustles of nature... she loved the absence of car engines and raised voices. Is this why her mother adored the countryside so much? Lucy had heard of people moving from the city to 'get away from it all,' but she was unsure why anyone would *want* to leave behind the conveniences of modern living... until that moment, when the clouds parted and rays of sunlight penetrated the forest, illuminating the ferns and leaves in beaming golden pockets. The dewy grass glistened, and even the cobwebs sparkled through the light dusting of mist that hovered over the ground. The effect wasn't eerie, or horrifying.

It was serene.

"This is dumb," she muttered, and as she gazed at the sky through the knotted branches, her lip trembled. "What the fuck?" she had time to say, before the tears came. Why? Was her city-girl brain ill-equipped to handle such overwhelming peacefulness?

It was ridiculous. She was crying over some trees.

"Fuck!" she roared, and laughed through her tears, for there was nobody around to stop her. *"Fuck!"* she shouted again. *"Piss! Balls! Tits!"* No one came out to admonish her, or to tell her to grow up.

She was all alone.

And she was free.

Brushing her hands through the ferns, she resumed her journey, breathing in the fresh scent as she kicked pine cones like a five-year-old. At that age, she had no worries, no cares in the world. She was young, and alive... and so was her mum.

"You would've loved it here," said Lucy, as something squelched underfoot. She looked down at the shallow pool of blood, and hurriedly stepped back. For the first time since entering the forest, she felt the insidious stirrings of fear. The pool was wide, and pieces of raw meat floated in it.

"Gross," she said.

You're in a forest, she told herself, as she gazed at the crimson splatters on a nearby tree trunk. *Animals kill and eat each other all the time.*

True, but something had really been butchered here.

Uneasily, she walked away from the slaughter, fixing her gaze dead ahead, where an unexpected sight had caught her eye. It appeared to be some sort of monument. She wandered closer, happy to leave the blood behind.

The domed structure, which stood around six feet tall, was crudely constructed from narrow stones. Words had been carved into the rock, but decades — centuries? — of erosion made them impossible to read. She trailed her fingers along the rough, moss-coated monument, and spotted another through the trees.

"Weird," she said, and ran to it. This one was identical in build, but less weathered, which allowed her to read the ancient lettering etched into the stone.

SEACHAD AIR A' PHUING SO THA CUNNART

"What the fuck language is that?"

She leaned against the structure, and when she pulled her hand away, it was wet and sticky and red. She wiped her fingers on the grass and looked up at the trail of fresh blood running down the pillar.

Fuck this. It was time to go home.

She backed away, heading for... wait, where was she? From which direction had she come? Everywhere she looked was the same; trees, trees, and more trees, the gnarled branches forming a ceiling above her. If she wanted to see, she'd have to climb, and there was no way in hell she was doing *that*.

She searched for her footprints, but her refusal to dirty her shoes meant she had left none. The trail was gone.

Fuck.

What to do? She remembered reading that anyone lost in the woods should find a stream and follow it. That was great advice — *terrific* fucking advice — if you happened to be lost next to a stream.

Breathe, breathe, she told herself. *Walk in one direction and see where it takes you.*

That sounded wise, so she followed her own instruction, treading further into — or hopefully *out* of — the woods. As she walked, she kept her eyes down, seeking a stray footprint, or some trace of the path. Finding none, she stopped and sipped her Irn-Bru.

The forest seemed darker than before.

Night couldn't have fallen already. She had been gone no more than an hour, surely. Packing her fizzy juice away, she kept going, humming her favourite songs to keep the gnawing dread at bay. She was halfway through Pearl Jam's *Ten* album when an icy wind whipped through the trees, the pine needles falling and scattering on the ground. The wind brought a curious sound with it.

Click-clack, click-clack.

"Is someone there?" It was a stupid thing to say, because that noise was anything but human. With her heart hammering in her chest, Lucy decided it was officially time to get the fuck out of here.

She turned and ran, not caring what direction she travelled in as long as it was away from that infernal, insect-like scuttling. Never one to excel in gym class — her lungs gave up at the merest suggestion of an incline — she was surprised at how fast her legs carried her. The sound got no louder, but she never slowed, her drink sloshing about in her schoolbag.

...click-clack...

...click-clack...

She spotted the path and joined it. Daylight forced its way through the canopy, and when she emerged from the woods into the clearing, she collapsed onto the grass, wheezing and panting, in a mixture of relief and exhaustion.

How long she lay there, she couldn't say, but when she managed to stand, and looked back at the forest — at the yawning chasm of darkness hidden beyond the treeline — she laughed.

"You're such an idiot."

What on earth had she thought was chasing her? A swarm of giant centipedes? She had gotten lost and freaked out like a big baby. She felt silly just thinking about it. Embarrassed, and tired, and hopelessly, utterly *silly*.

She rescued her frothy Irn-Bru from her bag and took a long drink, before heading home past the barn, her heart rate slowly returning to normal. Not once did she look back, even when she heard the strange rustling of the branches, because she knew nothing was there.

Absolutely... *nothing*.

Right?

No screams rang out from the forest that night, and in the morning, when Lucy stared out at the silent woods through her window, the drab sky rendered the landscape disappointingly prosaic.

How apt for her first day at a new school.

She was disappointed she hadn't died in her sleep, as that would have been the easiest way to avoid this grim new chapter of her life. But alive she was, and by the time her dad ambled downstairs to the breakfast table, she was showered and dressed and ready to go.

"You're up early," he said, failing to cover his mouth as he yawned. "It's only a short drive."

"I'm gonna walk to Helsbridge and get the school bus," said Lucy.

"You sure?" He plonked himself down on a chair and picked up a magazine. "It's your first day. I don't mind driving you."

"In a *van*? You want me to turn up at my new school in a van like I'm there to fix the plumbing?"

"Nothing wrong with being a plumber. There's good

money in the trades." Then, he muttered, "Wish I'd been a plumber."

She ignored him, and held up two earrings. "Hey, which ones say, *it's my first day at this school, but I'm really hip?*"

"The pair on the left."

"Thanks, dad," said Lucy, though she always remembered her mum's fashion advice; when it comes to jewellery or clothing, wear the opposite of what dad says. She placed the earrings he had chosen on the table and popped the other pair in. "What time does the bus pick me up?"

"It arrives in Helsbridge at eight-fifteen. Or is it eight-thirty?"

"So helpful."

"I know it stops by the war memorial." He glanced at her over the top of his magazine. "You sure you don't want a lift?"

"No."

She was lying, of course. The idea of walking onto a school bus was even more nerve-wracking than entering a new classroom. At least there, the teacher would show you to your seat. On the bus, she would have to hope there were spaces, or that she didn't end up accidentally sitting next to the school loser.

Unless that's you.

But she couldn't let her dad drop her off in a filthy van. Not on her first day, anyway. Once she was settled, and popular, she could take that risk. For now, she would get the bus like a normal person.

Normal is overrated.

Touché.

Before leaving, she checked herself in the mirror and thought she looked pretty in her black jeans and white shirt. As long as the school didn't have a policy against facial piercings, she'd be okay. Her nail polish had run out weeks ago, but she found a small tub of black paint her dad used for his model soldiers, and applied a couple of coats. She waggled her fingers, noting how the matte finish failed to catch the light.

Well, it was better than nothing.

The two-mile walk to Helsbridge along the edge of the forest took longer than expected, but she arrived in time for the bus, and by some miracle, the front seats were empty. She took one by the window, hoping someone would sit with her and introduce themselves so she wouldn't have to walk into school alone. They never did, so she sat and tried not to listen to the children whispering about her.

The school was bigger than she'd feared, and when the bus pulled into the car park, she got off and followed the signs to the head teacher's office. There, a woman handed her a timetable and escorted her to her first class, which was maths, and thankfully the teacher didn't make her stand in front of everyone and introduce herself. Her classmates were the usual mix of pretty girls and tall boys and the requisite class clown, though she didn't spot anyone who looked like they might be into Pearl Jam or Soundgarden.

Maths passed painlessly enough, and when the bell rang, Lucy checked her timetable and headed to her next class; art. Her teacher was a woman named Miss Wade, and Lucy took an instant liking to her. No matter the school, art teachers were always the coolest, closely followed by — for some reason — the geography teachers. With summer looming on the horizon, and the school year drawing to a close, Miss Wade put the radio on and told the class to do some sketches.

Lucy drew the strange monuments she had found in the woods from memory. Art was one of her best subjects, and she sketched methodically, recalling the curve of the rocks, the fuzzy moss and lichen that coated the stones, and the dark blood that—

"What's that you're drawing?"

She glanced up, and saw Miss Wade peering curiously at her work.

"Huh?" was all Lucy could say.

The teacher laughed softly. "I've not seen anything like them before."

Lucy's cheeks burned. "I, uh, saw them in the woods yesterday. Thought they were weird."

Miss Wade crouched by her side. "They *are* weird. But that's par for the course."

"Huh?"

Stop saying huh! She'll think that's all you can say.

Miss Wade didn't seem to mind. "There's a lot of weird stuff around these parts. I'm new here too, and every time I think I've seen it all, another oddity pops up."

"You live in Helsbridge?" Lucy found it hard to believe a professional woman like Miss Wade lived in a backwater place like Helsbridge, and she was absolutely right.

"No. I moved to Auchenmullan in January, and started here the same week. It's a nearby town. Bigger than Helsbridge, but just as weird." She smiled. "Where are you from?"

"Edinburgh."

"Wow. So quite the culture shock, right? Don't worry, you get used to it. The people here are nice. You'll make friends quickly."

Lucy wasn't sure about that, but she thanked Miss Wade and got back to her drawing. She wanted to talk some more, but if she was seen chatting to a teacher for too long, the other kids might think she was a creep.

Lunchtime rolled around, and at the sound of the bell, she packed up and followed the herd of hungry teenagers to the canteen, where a purple-cheeked dinner lady ladled meaty slop onto a plate with a cigarette in her mouth and her eyes half-shut.

Lucy balanced the unidentifiable grey rations and a can of Coke on her tray, and searched for a seat.

Where to go, where to go...

She noticed some girls from her maths class, and shuffled towards the lone empty chair at the table. Another girl swooped in before her, and Lucy swerved and kept walking. Laughter rang out behind her, but she couldn't tell if it was directed at her or not.

Don't be paranoid.

Shit. She couldn't see a spare seat anywhere, apart from one at a table of first year boys, and she refused to debase herself by sitting with—

"Hey, new girl!"

Wait. Did they mean her?

She turned towards a group of girls at a table. One of them signalled to her. "Over here!" The girl was pretty, with a 'Rachel' hairdo and a denim jacket with a Nirvana smiley face patch on the sleeve.

Nirvana?

At last, thought Lucy. *My people!*

She sped up, weaving through the tables and chairs while trying to keep the happy smile from her lips. "Hi, I'm Lucy," she said, as she laid her tray down beside the pretty girl and took a seat. "It's my—"

The girl plucked Lucy's Coke from her tray and opened it.

"—first day," Lucy finished.

"Cool," said the girl, taking a sip from Lucy's can and

placing it next to her own plate. "Okay, you can run along now."

Lucy didn't understand, so she sat there, smiling.

"Is she still there?" the girl asked her friends, and they laughed. Lucy laughed too, figuring it was better to be in on the joke.

"Come on, give it back," she smiled, reaching for the can.

The girl snatched it away. "The table service here is great," she said, and the other girls laughed again. It didn't take much, apparently. She turned to Lucy. "Oh my god, why are you still here?"

Lucy gestured towards the drink, and said, in a painfully small voice, "That's mine."

"What?"

"The drink. It's mine."

What are you doing? Everyone's looking at you!

"Forget it," she mumbled, and pushed her chair back. It made a groaning noise, and the girls giggled. Lucy grabbed her tray and started away from them.

"Hey," the pretty girl — who didn't *deserve* to wear a Nirvana patch — shouted. Lucy turned to face her. "Take your fucking drink with you." She threw the can, and out of pure instinct, Lucy reached to catch it, releasing her tray and letting it crash to the ground. The noise it made silenced the lunch hall, as the swill-like food splattered over her shoes. She caught the can, which would have been an impressive move, had it not sprayed Coca-Cola over her.

The worst part of the ordeal was the near-total silence that ensued as she stood there with cola dripping down her face and her lunch at her feet. Then someone laughed, and the entire hall joined in. A teacher approached — oh god, it was Miss Wade from art class! — and, with the hilarity ringing in her ears, she broke into a jog and barrelled through the doors, leaving the lunch hall behind. She ducked into the nearest toilets and found an empty cubicle, where she sat, trembling in shock.

"Great first impression, Lucy," she mumbled to herself. "Everyone's gonna want to be your friend *now*."

And yet, at that moment, it was her dad she hated more than anything. She hated him for making her move here, and for his inability to do his fucking job and write a book, and for forcing her to attend this school where it was only lunchtime and already she was the laughing stock of the canteen. How could she face her classmates again?

Once her tears dried up, she left the cubicle and scrubbed at the coke stains on her shirt with soap and water and handfuls of paper towels.

Her stomach rumbled, and she managed to find her way outside to where the bus had dropped her off that morning. Aside from a couple of kids smoking near the gate, it was quiet, and she sat on a low wall, wishing she'd brought a book. She hadn't, of course, because she'd worried someone would see her reading on her first day and think she was a loser.

So, how did that *work out for you?*

"Fuck off," she muttered, kicking her heels against the wall.

"I see ya met Isobel."

The voice surprised her. She had thought she was alone.

A bespectacled boy hopped up onto the wall beside her. "Mind if I sit?"

Lucy shrugged. "Whatever. I was just leaving."

"Wait a minute," he said. "Dinnae let Isobel ruin your day. This place isnae so bad."

She glanced wryly at him, and the boy laughed.

"Aye, so maybe it *is* that bad. But whatcha gonnae dae?

It's high school. It's supposed tae be shite, so that when we get old and start pissin' ourselves, we winnae look back and wish we were young, cos it wid mean going back tae school, dontcha think?"

Lucy wasn't sure what the hell he was talking about, so she just nodded. It seemed to placate him.

"The name's Rab, by the way," he said, and offered his hand.

She shook it, feeling very grown up. "Lucy. Nice to meet you."

"And dinnae mind Isobel, she's a right cunt." He burst out laughing. "It's okay, I can say that. She's ma sister."

"Your *sister*?"

"Aye. Folk cannae always tell, cos she puts on a plummy voice, but she's ma wee sister. She fuckin' hates me, like, and I hate her, but if you ignore her long enough, she'll go away."

"Did that work for you?"

"Fuck no. But I live in hope."

Lucy smiled, and looked at her feet.

"So, where you staying?" Rab asked. "Aviemore?"

"Helsbridge."

Rab nodded. "Helsbridge, whit a shiter. Sorry tae hear that. Helsbridge is pure crap."

"No kidding. We're not even in the town, we're in this random house a few miles away."

Rab looked her in the eyes for the first time. "Whit, the one next tae the forest?"

"Yeah. It's got all these scarecrows—"

"Aye, I ken it. *Everybody* kens it. You couldnae pay me tae live there."

"It could be worse," shrugged Lucy. "It only took me half-an-hour to walk to the bus this morning."

"I dinnae mean..." He trailed off, as realisation dawned on his face. "Holy shitebaws, you dinnae ken, eh?"

"Know what?" she said, aware of her own posh Edinburgh accent butting up against his broad Highland twang.

"Aye, of course your parents wouldnae tell ye."

"Then why don't you stop being a dick and tell me!"

He exhaled theatrically, and spoke with an aura of grave importance. "The kid that lived there — Bobby Chow — was *killed.*"

There it was. Vindication.

"I fucking knew something wasn't right," she said.

"No just that, though," Rab continued, leaning in for effect. "His family disappeared a week later. I heard they left aw their stuff behind and walked intae the forest." He paused. "And *naebody* ever saw them again."

A shiver ran through her. Feeling lightheaded, she jumped down from the wall in case she fell backwards. "What did you say?"

"Whit part?"

"All of it. Repeat everything you just said. Please."

"Uh, awright. Bobby Chow died, and—"

"You said he was *killed.*"

"Aye."

"By who?" Lucy's mind raced. Did her dad know about this?

"No by who," said Rab. "By *whit.*"

"Okay, then." She wished he'd get to the point. "By what?"

A broad grin stretched across his boyish face.

"Monsters," he said, with a knowing nod. "They were killed by big fuck-off *monsters.*"

8

"Shut up," said Lucy. She started away from Rab, and he jumped down after her.

"Wait, where ya going?"

"I've had enough of people making fun of me today, thank you."

He chased after her. "I'm no kidding!"

Lucy angrily spun to face him. "There's no such thing as monsters, you wee prick."

"Tell that to Bobby Chow's family."

"You're such a liar." And yet, something Rab had said played over in her mind.

They left aw their stuff behind and walked intae the forest.

In a twisted way, it made sense. Not the monsters part, but the family leaving after their son was murdered.

Murdered.

"I'm no lying," Rab insisted in a petulant tone. Lucy guessed he was older than her, probably seventeen or eighteen. An unreliable age for a boy. "Kids used tae disappear aw the time round here, and since Grace Lewis's wee sister died, and then Bobby Chow, everyone's parents are freakin' out. They say it's startin' again."

"You're full of shit," said Lucy. "I mean, what kind of monsters? Bigfoot? Nessie?"

"Dunno. Nae one's seen them. But we aw ken tae avoid the woods, especially at night. If ya hear the screams, stay inside and lock—"

"What screams?" A chill skated down her spine.

"The screams," said Rab. "I heard 'em once, earlier this year, before everything went wrong. It sounded like a girl, but..."

"But what?"

"I'm no sure. It sounds daft, like, but I thought it was somethin' trying tae *sound* like a girl, you ken whit I mean?" He pushed his glasses further up the bridge of his nose. "Look, I didnae mean tae scare you. I'm just telling you tae be careful around the woods. Best tae avoid them altogether." He smiled. "I dinnae want you tae disappear before we even get a *chance* tae be pals."

If Rab's goal had been to frighten her, the little pipsqueak had succeeded, and she hated him for it. Still, she couldn't hate him too much, because right now, he was the closest thing she had to a friend.

No one else spoke to her that day, and if they had, she wouldn't have noticed, as she spent her remaining classes thinking about Rab's story. The whole business with the monsters didn't concern her, because that was clearly bollocks. But the kid dying? Or being murdered?

That was plausible.

As for his family disappearing by walking into the forest,

they had certainly abandoned their home and all their belongings, so perhaps there was a morsel of truth in there, too. She wanted to talk to someone about it, but there was only her dad, or possibly Miss Wade, and she didn't want her favourite teacher to think she was a nutter.

I thought it was somethin' trying tae sound like a girl.

God, that was the worst part. She *had* heard screams that first night... or something that sounded like them.

You're being a dope. Don't let some stupid folk tale get in your head.

But what about the monuments she found in the forest?

What about them?

And the blood!

Again, so what?

She was still thinking about it when the bell rang and ended the day. Lucy ambled out of the school, letting the other teens shove past her, and walked towards the waiting bus. It was painted yellow like the ones in America, and hard to miss against the grey buildings and the sea of white cars. The teens shuffled on one-by-one, including—

"Oh, *come on,*" Lucy sighed.

There, getting on her bus, was the bitch with the Nirvana patch.

Isobel.

Dammit, did she live in Helsbridge? Would they share the school bus twice a day? Lucy couldn't bear the thought of further humiliation, so she stood helplessly by as the doors wheezed shut and the bus drove off, leaving her standing in the car park.

What now?

She had missed her ride, but it was a nice day, and the sun was pleasantly warm, so she decided a long walk would be the best way to clear her head.

It's not like her dad would notice if she was late.

With a last look back at the school, she set off. The journey home —with the exception of one steep hill — was reasonably flat, and there were no turnoffs to confuse her other than the occasional muddy track leading to a farm. The persistent stench of cow shit turned her stomach, but she imagined that, in time, she would get used to it.

Please god, let me get used to it.

A couple of cars passed by, and one tractor — the farmer waved at her, and she waved back — but otherwise the road was quiet. Birds cheeped melodically in the trees, and for a while, she managed to forget all about Isobel and the dead boy who had lived in her house by simply enjoying the sounds of nature, and feeling the sun on her face. God, she was turning into a real nerd.

Her mum would be proud.

By the time she reached Helsbridge, the sun had dipped behind the clouds, and her legs were tiring. This was the most exercise she'd had in over a year, and if she kept this up, her poor trainers wouldn't last the—

A sharp scream echoed from nearby.

Lucy stopped and peered into the woods.

The scream came again, and she realised her mistake. What she heard was laughter; a proper witch's cackle. Lucy believed in witches as much as she believed in monsters, so she abandoned the path and trod into the forest.

The drop in temperature hit her immediately.

Be careful around the woods, Rab had warned her. *Best tae avoid them altogether.*

Yeah, but since when had anyone trusted teenage boys?

"Monsters," she chuckled, and strode further into the forest. Another peal of laughter echoed. Yeah, that was no monster. That was a girl. Lucy crept forwards, stepping carefully through the vegetation, until she heard hushed voices whispering behind a fallen tree.

Should she introduce herself? Or act casual, as if she just happened to be passing by as she walked home through the woods? Neither option felt natural.

Go talk to them. What's the worst that could happen?

Her mind whirred with endless possibilities. A bush rustled ahead of her.

They'll see you. Don't just stand there!

She started forwards as a red-haired girl stood from behind the fallen trunk.

"Who's there?" the girl asked, a cigarette clutched between her fingers. Before Lucy could reply, the girl laughed. "Oi Izzy, you'll never believe who's spying on us."

Izzy.

It only took Lucy one second to put it together, but it was one second too long.

"Oh, fuck," she said, and started to run.

9

───────

Lucy didn't get far.

She was already knackered from the walk, and wasn't used to running through forests. Or running at all, for that matter. Footsteps rapidly gained on her, the two girls laughing as they gave chase, and then someone shoved her and Lucy hit the dirt, sprawling across the forest floor.

"I got the bitch!"

"Hold her down!" said Isobel, and the red-haired girl threw herself atop Lucy, pressing her face into the soggy pine needles.

Isobel took her by the hair and lifted her head. The girl stared at her like they were mortal enemies. "What the fuck are you doing here?" she asked, then took a swig from a bottle of vodka. "Are you spying on us, new girl?"

Lucy spat out a mouthful of pine needles. "No. I... I heard voices, that's all. I just came to see who it was."

Isobel turned to her friend. "So, she was spying on us."

"Sounds like it," the red-haired girl said. "Probably watching us wi' her hand down her pants, frigging herself silly."

"I wasn't!" shouted Lucy. She struggled to free herself, but the girl pulled her arm behind her back, raising it higher until the pain forced her to stop.

"Who even *are* you?" asked Isobel. "And why won't you leave me alone?"

"She's pure obsessed wi' you," said her friend.

"My name's Lucy," she said, and started to cry. "I'm sorry I bothered you. I just want to go home."

"What, you think we can let you leave? So you can tell our parents you caught us drinking?"

Lucy hated the maniacal gleam in Isobel's eyes. "I won't, I promise," she sobbed. "I don't know your parents. I don't even know who you are!"

"Oh, you will," said Isobel. She snatched the cigarette from her friend. "I'm Isobel, and that's Judith. We basically run Kingussie High School." Under different circumstances, Lucy would have found the threat laughable. But outnumbered two-to-one in a forest, it sent a pang of fear through her.

"Please, let me go. I'm sorry, and I won't tell anyone, I swear."

"You promise?"

"I promise!" She wished she wasn't crying.

"Okay," said Isobel. "I believe you. But we can't let you go without paying the toll, can we?"

"I don't have any money," said Lucy, and it was true. She had spent the paltry amount she brought to school on a lunch she never even got to taste.

Isobel nodded. "I see. No money, huh? That's a bummer." A sly grin crossed her face. "Guess we'll have to take something else."

Lucy didn't understand. What did—

"Judith, get her shoes."

"Oh my god, amazing," said Judith, as she shuffled around atop Lucy.

"Stop! Please!" she cried, powerless to prevent the girl from pulling her trainers from her feet. In desperation, she cried, "I'm friends with your brother!"

"What, Rab?" asked Isobel.

"Yes! We spoke at lunchtime!"

"Fine. In that case," Isobel added with a laugh, "take her socks too!"

"I'm no' touching her sweaty feet!" said Judith.

"Fucking do it!"

Nails scratched at Lucy's ankles as the girl rolled her socks down and yanked them off. "Give them back!" She didn't want to tell them they were her last pair of shoes. It would only make things worse.

The pressure on her spine alleviated as Judith got off her. Lucy scrambled to her bare, wet feet. They sank into the needles, mud squelching between her toes.

"Oh my god," laughed Judith. "Look at her! Look at the new girl!"

"She's so cool," sneered Isobel, methodically tying Lucy's laces together into a tight knot. She held the shoes out, letting them dangle from her fingers. "Now, let's see how high we can get these." She whirled them around her head like a medieval weapon and launched Lucy's trainers through the air.

"Oh fuck," laughed Judith. She was practically doubled over in hilarity. "Did they even land?"

"What are you waiting for?" Isobel shouted in Lucy's face. "Go find them!"

There was no point arguing. She was at their mercy now. Onwards she walked, her feet sinking into the foul mud with each step, tears streaming down her face. She didn't think her day could get any worse.

She was wrong.

"There they are!" said Judith, and Lucy looked up to see her trainers swinging gently from a branch high above her.

"Aw shite, it's like the Auchenmullan shoe tree," roared Isobel, and she and Judith dissolved into hysterics. Lucy had no idea what they were talking about, nor did she care. Her shoes were out of reach. What would she tell her dad? They couldn't afford another pair, and the ones left behind by the Chow family were so big she'd have to stuff them with newspaper and walk around like a clown.

She *needed* her trainers.

Judith clapped her on the shoulder. "Sucks tae be you, eh?"

That was not new information. It *did* suck to be Lucy Brannigan.

She walked towards the tree, sizing up the narrow trunk and spindly branches. It wouldn't be a difficult climb — the branches were frequent and well-spaced — but it was high, and she was not convinced the thin limbs would hold her weight. She grabbed one and shoogled it. Then, without pausing to consider whether this was a good idea, Lucy began her ascent, sticking as close to the trunk as possible, where she figured the branches would be strongest.

"Look, she's going up!" said Judith. "Like a wee fucking monkey!"

She ignored them, concentrating on moving her poor, sockless feet from branch to jagged branch. The boughs groaned under the pressure.

Come on, come on.

A small missile whistled past her head. The bullies were throwing pine cones at her. They pinged off her legs and bum, and one whacked her on the head. Despite the barrage, she continued to climb.

"Stop it!" she shouted, as she looked down at them in anger.

Christ, she was higher than anticipated, and the height made her swoon. Her stomach dropped, and she rested all her weight on one foot, causing the branch to snap. She screamed, and moved both hands to the same branch, one leg dangling over nothing. She hugged her body to the tree, her cheek scraping against the bark, kicking her leg out until it found a place to rest. Were they... were they trying to make her fall? It might not kill her, but she'd likely break something.

The girls resumed throwing their pine cones, and Lucy continued climbing. Her shoes were almost within reach. She just had to get... a little... higher...

She shuffled her foot along a branch that looked sturdier than the rest. Would it be strong enough? Only one way to find out. Holding on with one hand, she placed both feet on the branch and stretched her arm towards her shoes. It groaned beneath her, bending at an alarming angle.

"Hey, that's not gonna hold," someone said from far below, but she couldn't stop now.

Her fingertips brushed the shoelaces.

She was so... so...

Got them!

She closed a fist around the laces, sliding the trainers towards her along the branch...

And then came the scream.

It was the same as the other night; high-pitched and girlish and slightly alien. Lucy looked down at the bullies. Already, they were backing nervously away.

"Shit," she heard Judith say. *"Fucking run!"*

Another scream.

Whatever it was, it was getting closer.

Lucy yanked the shoelaces, sending her trainers hurtling through the air. They landed on the forest floor, and — suddenly gripped by terror — she began her frenzied descent, half-climbing and half-falling down the tree. She placed her feet carelessly on the slippery branches, scratching her hands and face.

Click-clack, click-clack.

She looked to her left, deeper into the forest, and saw movement.

"Fuck," she said, and in her hysteria, put her foot where she thought — or hoped — a branch would be.

It wasn't there.

For a moment, Lucy was weightless in free-fall. Then she hit a branch and it spun her, turning her head-over-heels. She smacked her hip, then her skull, before slamming hard onto the ground.

Click-clack, click-clack.

She tried to crawl, but her body wouldn't respond. Her woozy vision swam in and out of focus.

The ground rumbled as a colossal, violent roar boomed throughout the forest.

It was the last thing Lucy heard before she blacked out completely.

10

───────

Lucy had always been jealous of people who remembered their dreams.

Her dad used to transfer his to the page, turning those illusory fragments into stories, until one day — or so he claimed — he stopped dreaming altogether.

Now, Lucy didn't believe *anyone* ever stopped dreaming, but according to him, he simply forgot how, which made her sad. She figured it happened when her mum died. A lot of things changed around that time.

Her dad tried to make out everything was fine, but sometimes, late at night when he thought she was asleep, she heard him crying through the walls. She told him once that he didn't have to pretend, and he got mad and sent her to her room. He was trying to shield her from the real world and all its myriad disappointments, but he needn't have bothered.

She knew them all too well, for her mum's death had destroyed her.

It had been two years now, and not a day passed when she didn't miss her. Even though they had constantly argued, it never mattered. That was just what kids and their parents did. They fought, and then they made up, ready to quarrel another day. It never meant they didn't love each other. On the contrary, it only strengthened their bond.

But despite the loss of her mother, life had continued on. After a while, she was even expected to go back to school and learn about useless pursuits like algebra and chemistry. How the hell was she supposed to concentrate on her future when she knew how quickly it could be ripped away? Her dad got a bit odd around that time, too. Eccentric, would be the polite, quintessentially British way to put it. She thought he was trying to make up for her mum's absence by acting like Father of the Year, when all she really wanted was her old dad back.

And that was what Lucy had been dreaming of when she woke up; her mum and dad, the three of them together again, running through the forest as fire blazed all around them. Brief snippets of the vision hovered out of reach for a while, and then faded forever.

She was awake.

Her head ached like hell, and it hurt to open her eyes, so she didn't bother. Instead, she stretched, and rubbed her cranium. Her fingers found a lump, and she winced at the touch. She could move, though, and nothing *felt* broken. She tested each arm and leg, raising and lowering them, then worked every finger and toe. All the relevant parts appeared to be in working order.

"Not dead yet," she said, and opened her eyes.

Something jabbed into her spine, and she moved onto her hands and knees to inspect her surroundings. She was in a shallow pit of sticks and twigs and soft, leafy branches, like a bird's nest, but large enough to comfortably fit a dozen adults. Majestic tree limbs lined with golden leaves swayed hypnotically above her, buffeted by a strong wind that whipped her hair across her face.

This was not where she had fallen.

She crawled up the gentle incline and peered over the lip of the bowl.

"Oh, fuck me," she said.

She was up a tree.

Her stomach lurched. She overlooked the treetops, where, in the distance, she spotted the clearing where her dad was probably sitting typing in his office. Beyond that, smoke rose from the chimneys of Helsbridge's cottages and farmhouses.

How the hell did she get up here? There had to be steps, or a ladder. She leaned further over the edge, but, on this side, the branches appeared to be the only way up.

Her shoes and schoolbag were lying on a pile of leaves. Afraid to stand, and with twigs stabbing into her palms and knees, she made her way over. The laces were still tied together, so she undid them and slipped the shoes on over her dirty, bare feet, happy to be reunited with her footwear. It was a small, but welcome, victory.

Figuring there *must* be a way down, she crawled to the opposite side of the nest. From this angle, the forest seemed to go on forever. Her gaze lingered on several large patches where the trees had turned black. No leaves clung to the diseased trunks, as if the areas had been ravaged by fire, or somehow gone bad.

"I want to go home," she whispered.

Gripping onto the nest, she leaned over the side. Once again, no steps, and no ladders. Just scrawny branches and long indentations that scarred the trunk from top to bottom.

Claw marks.

Lucy trembled.

Something had climbed up here. A creature with huge, savage talons.

Primordial terror rose within her as she remembered the roar she had heard before losing consciousness.

"Help!" she shouted. *"Somebody help me, please!"* Her voice echoed through the valley. But who was around to hear?

A bird flew from a tree and took to the air, heading towards the faraway mountains. What if no one came? She couldn't jump, that was for sure. Not without breaking every bone in her body. But the branches might hold her...?

She looked again, trying not to dwell on the deep trenches from the creature's claws.

The monster...

"There's no such thing," she said.

And then she saw it.

The large, dark shape.

It lumbered through the woods, cracking branches from trees and crashing through the undergrowth. Too far away to get a true sense of its size, she recalled the mysterious form on the edge of the forest that first day, and suddenly — far, far too late — she understood the purpose of the scarecrows.

There *was* a monster in Helsbridge... and she was trapped in its lair.

That's stupid. There's no such thing as—

The monster emerged from the shadows, and Lucy gasped in horror. The stout, fur-coated body moved like a bear, skewering the ground with enormous, bony nails as it stalked towards the tree.

"Oh god," she breathed.

It was coming home.

The great beast reared up, thrusting its savage hooks

into the bark. Lucy ducked back into the nest, her brain clouding with fear. Where could she go? Her chest constricted. She was hyperventilating. Should she jump? Was that preferable to being torn apart?

She scrambled to the edge, fighting against the gale, and stared out, daring herself to take a leap into the unknown. Bile rose in her throat as she shuffled closer. She heard the monster's claws gouging into the tree, and imagined the damage they would do to her soft, pink flesh.

Jump.

No.

Aim for the nearest tree.

It was too far. She'd never make it. To jump now would be suicidal.

And so, with no other options available, Lucy turned to face her destiny. A burly paw the size of her head appeared over the side of the nest, and she dropped to her knees.

"Please," she sobbed, as if she could reason with a blood-thirsty beast. "Don't kill me."

A second paw came into view, and when the monster's head rose behind the packed twigs and branches, Lucy closed her eyes and thought of her father.

"I'm sorry," she whispered.

Why couldn't she have been kinder to him? He was only trying his best, yet all she did was complain. She wasn't the only one hurting. She couldn't imagine — hadn't even *tried* to imagine — how he must feel. And now he was about to lose his only daughter. Would they ever find her remains? Would there be anything left? She recalled the pool of blood she had stepped in. Was that to be her fate?

The beast grunted, and Lucy shook her head, refusing to open her eyes.

"Come on, then," she said, in a final defiant act of

teenage rebellion. "Eat me, you bastard. But I hope you fucking *choke*."

Another grunt. The monster was toying with her.

"Do it!" she roared. *"Fucking kill me!"*

It padded across the nest and stopped, its odious breath seething against her skin. A wet tongue slapped against her cheek, and Lucy braced herself for a mouthful of razor-sharp teeth to clamp down on her face and tear it off.

The creature licked her.

An interminable minute passed. The big brute snorted. Then, she heard it turn and wander away, each step causing the nest to shake.

With slobbery drool dripping down her cheek, Lucy opened one eye.

The monster sat opposite her on its voluminous rear end, its legs splayed out.

She opened her other eye.

The creature held a twisted branch to its mouth, tearing off leaves and chewing them noisily, clear sap running down its hairy chin.

Lucy took in the extraordinary sight. With its long snout and squat, barrel-like body, the beast reminded her of one of those huge guinea pigs she had seen on telly. What were they called?

Capybaras.

Yes, that was it.

The claws it had used to scale the tree had retracted into the furry paws. Only the tips remained, with which the monster clutched the branch.

It noticed her looking, and offered her the snack.

"No, thank you," she croaked, and the creature went back to its meal.

Lucy sat for what felt like hours, watching the oversized

rodent eat. Once finished, the monster tossed the stripped branch onto the nest, and turned its attention to Lucy.

"What are you?" she asked.

Black, lazy eyes looked at her vacantly.

"Did you bring me here?"

Again, nothing. It sat like a gnome, its nose twitching. Was this the monster feared by the town? This... this big *goof?* There was no way it was responsible for the deaths. For a start, it was obviously vegetarian.

The beast clambered onto all fours, and Lucy scooted backwards. The monster paused, eyeing her cautiously, and rolled onto its back with a playful grunt.

She didn't move. "You..." — the words sounded ridiculous coming from her lips — "...you want a belly rub?"

With a hand that would not stop trembling, Lucy reached for the monster and ran her hand through his fur. The creature snorted in satisfaction as Lucy scratched his tummy.

She laughed.

"You're not gonna eat me, are you?" She rubbed his belly more vigorously. "You don't want to kill me! You're a big silly guy, aren't you?" He felt good to pet, like a giant teddy bear whose smooth hairs brushed against her palms and eased her anxiety. She closed her eyes and leaned against him.

Him?

Well, she thought so. It's not like she could ask, and it was rude to look.

"You live here, huh? All by yourself?" She gazed up at the darkening sky. It was getting late. "Hey," she said. "I need to get home." The creature looked at her. "You know that word? *Home?*"

He sighed, and — with great effort — rolled onto his front, causing the nest to shift alarmingly. Lucy lost her balance, stumbling against him, and he scooped her up with one mighty paw.

"Woah!" she said, as her feet left the ground. Before she could say anything more intelligent, he was carrying her towards the edge of the nest. With one bound, they plunged over the side. The sudden drop stole Lucy's voice, and her mouth opened in a silent scream as the pair spun out-of-control towards another tree. Lucy braced herself, but, like Gene Kelly on a lamppost, the monster swung around it and spiralled to the bottom.

Lucy's lungs caught up with her, but the ensuing scream was the excitable roar of a kid on a rollercoaster rather than a shriek of terror. They came to a stop, and the next thing she knew, her feet were on solid ground. She stumbled backwards, dizzily falling onto her arse and giggling. Her heart raced from the rapid descent. She couldn't believe such a — how to put it delicately — *fat little monster* could be so agile. He reminded her of that actor her dad liked, the one from all those kung-fu films he used to watch. Not Jackie Chan, the other one... Sammo something.

"Sammo," she said, and pointed at him. The monster plonked itself down. The ground trembled as he did so. "I'm going to call you *Sammo.*"

As expected, he said nothing. She wondered if he understood a word she was saying. With her dizzy spell abating, she got to her feet. "Sorry, I have to go now." She looked around at the identical trees. "Uhh... which way is my home?"

Sammo tilted his head slightly.

"This way?" asked Lucy, following his gaze. "My home is this way?"

Sammo had nothing to add.

"Okay. I'll go that way." She started off, then turned back to him. "Can I see you again?"

The big capybara stared at her. Then, Sammo's mouth stretched into something approximating a grin. Lucy realised he was copying her, and she ran and threw her arms around him.

"Thank you," she said, before letting go and racing through the woods. She couldn't stop smiling. How was this real? No one would ever believe her... and that was fine. She didn't want to tell a soul. Sammo was her friend.

Friend?

Sure. Why not? Her first day of school, and she had made a friend. Okay, so he was a giant monster who lived in a nest, but who cares?

A friend was a friend... and that was all that mattered.

By the time Lucy arrived home, the sun was low.

She navigated the field of scarecrows and found the front door unlocked. Her dad was really getting into this whole 'country life' business.

She dumped her schoolbag by the door and took two paracetamol to ease the pain in her neck, then hopped in the shower to make herself presentable. Dirt and blood streamed down her legs, and afterwards, she wrapped herself in a towel and stared into the mirror, wiping away the steam.

One eye was badly bruised, and a thin cut marred her forehead.

"Dammit," she said, pressing a finger to the purple mark around her eye. There was no way to hide it. All she could do was pray no one looked at her in school tomorrow, which was, sadly, entirely possible.

She left the bathroom and took the stairs up to her bedroom. The house was quiet. Too quiet. Was her dad home? She snuck along the hallway to his writing room and peered in at him. There he sat, gazing at his typewriter while his hands fidgeted with an elastic band.

Lucy shuffled back out of sight, then noisily stomped her feet on the floor. "Dad, I'm home," she shouted.

At the sound of her voice, he began hammering the keys. "Great! How was school?"

"Rubbish. I'm never going back."

"That's my girl."

"You eaten?"

"Not yet. Been working hard all day."

She poked her head around the door. "Oh yeah? Progress on the new book?"

"Absolutely. The words are flowing today. Can't seem to stop!"

She wished he wouldn't lie to her. "That's great, dad."

"Yeah, I'll have this one finished in no time."

She balled her fists. "Want me to put something on for tea?"

"That'd be smashing. Just wrapping up this chapter, and I'll be down in a jiffy."

She started to speak, but the words caught in her throat. She took a breath, and sniffed back tears. "Cool. I'm gonna get dressed. See you down there."

"You're the best," he shouted.

She retreated to her bed, where she sat and cried. She wasn't angry with her dad for lying. It had been a long, crazy day, that was all, and what she needed was dinner and a sleep. She gazed out the window as she put her pyjamas on.

The trees blew gently, and she wondered whatever became of her poor, stolen socks. She'd no doubt have to face Isobel and Judith again tomorrow, and with one hell of a shiner.

Ah, fuck 'em.

She placed her palm against the cool glass.

"Goodnight, Sammo," she said, and went downstairs. She supposed that, tomorrow, she would find out whether this had all been a dream or not. But for now, she had dinner to make... monsters or no monsters.

11

———————

IT TURNED OUT THE PREVIOUS DAY HAD NOT BEEN A DREAM.

The swollen purple eye that gazed back at Lucy from the bedroom mirror was testament to that. She looked at herself with a mixture of horror and revulsion, which was not unusual, but at least this time she had good reason. After quietly dressing, she crept to her dad's room and put her ear to the door.

He was snoring.

Perfect.

She wasn't going to school today. How could she concentrate after yesterday's events? This was more important than trigonometry; more important even than *art*.

She threw together a couple of ham sandwiches and snuck out the front door, racing through the long grass with her schoolbag bouncing against her spine, eager to run her fingers through Sammo's fur and search for meaning in his small, drowsy eyes.

Excitement built in her stomach. She wanted to shout, to call his name.

Not yet!

She couldn't wake her dad.

The light drizzle was refreshing on her sleepy face, and once she entered the forest and ran beneath the thick blanket of leaves, she heard the rain rather than felt it. A low mist swirled around her feet, dispersing as she stepped through. The trees smelt different today. Sweeter. Or maybe her improved mood heightened her senses?

"Sammo? You there? It's me, Lucy."

Did he know her name? Had she even introduced herself? She strode on. This was *much* better than stupid old school, and though the woods were dark, she was unafraid. She looked up at the mighty trunks, searching for the tell-tale claw marks, or the golden foliage of Sammo's nest. She was surprised monsters lived in nests. Perhaps he liked to gaze up at the stars?

Further she went, beyond the strange monuments, making sure to not get turned around. She needed a compass. Surely she could pick one up in Helsbridge, or borrow one from the school geography department? Then she could walk as far as she liked without fear of getting lost.

The rain grew heavier, bleeding through the branches, so she sheltered beneath a tree and ate her first sandwich. A full stomach was important for adventuring, she reasoned, and she thought about what else might be useful for investigating the forest. Waterproofs were top of her list. What about a ball of string? She could tie it to a tree and use it to find her way back.

Yes! That was a great idea.

"Sammo? You there?"

Where *was* he? Still asleep? She wondered what hours monsters kept. It's not like they had to be up early for school. If they wanted, she bet they could sleep for twenty hours a day. Wouldn't that be—

Click-clack.

Lucy paused.

That sound… she had heard it before, when she had run for her life that first time in the forest. She laughed. God, she had almost peed herself that day. Well, she wouldn't act like a baby again. She would investigate the noise, because that's what she was now; an explorer. Nothing would deter her.

Except maybe the screams.

Click-clack.

She followed the sound.

"Sammo?"

It could be him. She imagined his claws clicking together as he lumbered through the forest.

"Sammo! It's me!"

On she jogged, deeper into the woodland, no longer paying attention to where she ran. She passed blackened trees with drooping limbs, their withered branches inter-twining, and skipped over the dry, frazzled ground.

At last, she slowed. Something wasn't right. She recalled the patches of dead forest visible from Sammo's nest, and as she stopped and glanced around, she realised she was in one of them. Scorch marks disfigured the trunks, and no foliage hung from the spindly, decaying branches.

…click-clack, click-clack…

And there, encircled by cadaverous saplings, was a hole in the ground.

…click-clack, click-clack…

The noise was coming from inside.

Lucy crept over. The hole was wide — about three feet — but there was no way Sammo could squeeze in. She moved closer and peered down. Darkness swallowed the end of the tunnel, but Lucy had come prepared. She pulled a torch from her schoolbag and aimed into the pit. Glassy white fluid trickled down the walls, and she ran the beam across them until the tunnel curved out of sight.

...click-clack...

From deep within, something stirred.

"Sammo...?" she whispered.

No.

...click-clack...

That wasn't him.

...click-clack, click-clack...

Lucy backed away. The trees seemed closer than before, and with them, they brought overwhelming darkness. Where had she come from? She spun, the torch keeping the shadows at bay.

...click-clack, click-clack, click-clack...

The noise made her skin crawl.

Go. Just go.

Good idea. She started walking, not caring where as long as it was away from this awful place. The dead trees fenced her in, and she squeezed between them. Above her, branches shook. One snapped.

Lucy kept going. She shouldn't have come this far.

Something scratched her cheek, and she screamed.

A branch, it was only a—

The ground gave way beneath her.

She threw out her hands, grabbing hold of a branch as she dropped. The bough bent as her legs kicked helplessly over another tunnel.

Her desperate fingers slid along the tree limb.

"No!" she screamed, trying to dig her toes into the tunnel's hard, earthen walls. She slipped further, panic building.

"Help me!"

The branch groaned, bending further than it should. Lucy gripped it with one hand, using the other to search for plants or roots, something, *anything* to hold on to.

Then the dry wood snapped, and Lucy Brannigan's whole world went impossibly dark.

12

———

Lucy hooked her nails, gouging trenches into the walls as she slid down the pit. She spread her legs apart, gaining traction with her feet, until she managed to slow herself to a complete stop.

The torch had dropped from her fingers and rolled around a bend. It lay out of sight, lighting the narrow tunnel below her.

"Oh god, oh god." The hole was narrower than the previous one, and she kept herself up by pressing her feet and back against opposing walls. How far had she fallen? She looked up, and a frightened whimper escaped her lips.

Too far.

She had to get out. She had to get out before she lost her fucking mind.

Climb.

But she was secure right now. If she climbed, she risked slipping further into the tunnel.

So what are you gonna do, stay here?

She felt sick. Tentatively, she placed one foot higher,

then shimmied her back, stabbing her fingertips into the earth for good measure.

There. She had moved a couple of centimetres. That was progress, wasn't it? Sweat dripped down her forehead. Why was it so hot in here? She clawed at the dirt, nudging herself higher. Her breath came in short gasps.

"Come on, *come on.*"

There was no hurry. She didn't need to rush. The important thing was getting out of here, and—

...click-clack, click-clack...

Fuck.

She waited. Was it coming from—

...click-clack, click-clack...

Yes. It was.

Don't freak out.

Too late. Full-blown terror erupted inside her gut.

Something was in here with her.

Lucy climbed faster. She closed her eyes, placing one foot above the other, going higher and higher at an infinitesimally slow pace.

"Please, please," she sobbed. One foot slid, and she jammed her other heel into the dirt, pausing for only a second before resuming her climb. She looked down at the torchlight.

...click-clack, click-clack...

The dreadful sound grew louder, closer.

A shadow obscured the beam.

"Fuck!" she roared.

Cool air tickled her face.

Almost there.

The light strobed below her as the dark shape passed through it.

Click-clack, click-clack.

She poked her head above the surface and pivoted, grasping frenziedly at the ground, pushing herself up and out.

A scream echoed from below.

She didn't look down.

Instead, she dragged herself out of the tunnel and scrambled to her feet, taking off through trees lit by slender dapples of fading daylight. Faces leered at her from the grizzled trunks, and she barrelled between them.

That scream again.

So human-like.

She looked over her shoulder and saw nothing. But she heard it.

God, she heard it.

Something yanked her backwards. Her jacket... it was snagged on something. She took a step back, and felt pressure behind her, tough material affixing itself to her clothes.

What the fuck? She couldn't move!

The sticky substance clung to her like a snare, fastening tightly to her arms and legs. Thin cords seemed to bind her, and she tried in vain to pull free. A net? Who would leave a fucking net out here in the...

Oh god.

The truth sank in.

That was no net.

Oh Jesus Christ.

It was a web.

"No, no," she whimpered.

The white threads dripped with a vile ooze that reeked of shit, and every movement seemed to draw the strands tighter across her limbs. She tried to wrench her arm loose, succeeding only in becoming more entangled. The acrid slime dribbled down her arms and face. It burned. She thrashed her body, the bond strengthening.

Within the gnarled branches, a light gleamed.

Stay back, she wanted to command, but her voice deserted her as the lurking presence stepped out of the shadows.

At last, Lucy found the strength to scream.

Eight legs uncurled from between the trees, followed by two crab-like claws attached to sinewy arms protruding from a bulbous, fleshless body. Atop it, a pulsing, transparent sac inflated, revealing a membranous tentacled horror floating inside. The obscene sac flared a fluorescent pink, lighting up the surrounding area and making the web glow as it tightened across Lucy's flailing limbs.

Like a funnel-web spider emerging from its lair, the monster stalked towards her. Liquid dribbled onto Lucy's head, and she looked up.

She shouldn't have.

A second monster clambered down the web, salivating from a small, puckered orifice below the pink cyst. She was going to die, and the only reason she hadn't yet lost her mind was because her fucking brain kept repeating, *now, that is a monster.*

"Leave me alone!"

The first creature raised its claws, and as the jellied sac inflated once more, the floating nightmare inside vibrated, and that hideous scream that had awoken her on her first night in Helsbridge resonated throughout the forest.

Then... it was gone.

Out of the darkness leapt Sammo, slamming into the monster, the pair tumbling across the cracked and brittle ground. Lucy tried to turn her head, but the movement almost ripped the webbed hair from her scalp. All she could do was listen, until the monster hurtled into view and slammed against a tree. It dropped, then flipped itself onto its eight legs. Sammo was on him instantly. The huge rodent, with his round body and graceless posture, hacked and slashed with bared claws, gouging out strings of fetid intestines. The dying monster closed its pincer over Sammo's wrist and clamped down. Blood bubbled from the wound, and Sammo responded by opening his mouth and biting the monster's arm. He shook his head back and forth, the inhuman flesh tearing between his jaws. Black blood frothed from the torn limb, spilling down Sammo's fur, and he sank his claws into the wet, pink sac, ripping it asunder.

"Get him, Sammo!" shouted Lucy. It was all she could do. "Kill him!"

The dry bushes behind him rustled, and before he could react, a new fiend thudded onto Sammo's back, wrapping its legs around him.

Putrid ooze slopped onto Lucy's scalp. She glanced at the creature above her.

"Sammo! *There's another one!*"

He looked at her, as the monster on his back ground its limbs into his torn flesh. Then the second fiend sprang from the web. Sammo tried to keep the creature at bay, but it latched on, pincers biting and snapping at his face. They sliced his snout open, unleashing another flood of crimson blood. Sammo clawed at the swollen pink cyst on the monster's body, but it deflated before he could snag it.

He was outnumbered. Lucy needed to help, but the web prevented her from—

Wait. *She* wasn't stuck to it. Her clothes were.

Idiot!

Her arms were too close to her sides to easily slip out of

her jacket. She would have to unfasten it. One sleeve was fully caught, but the other was free from the elbow down, and she reached across her body, fingers groping desperately for the zipper. The metal pull was tantalisingly out of reach.

Sammo scratched and tore at the monster in front of him, helpless to do anything about the beast on his back. His fur was turning a dark red.

"I'm coming," Lucy grunted, straining her arm to reach the zipper. She pinched the toggle between the tips of her fingers and tugged it down until the jacket opened. She slipped one arm loose, but her other hand was caught on the web. With a yell of pain, she wrenched it free, removing several layers of skin in the process.

"Fuck!" she cried.

With her arms unburdened, she unbuckled her belt and fell forwards, sliding out of her baggy jeans and landing with a thump on the ground.

Ahead, Sammo spun in a bloody circle. The warm fluid splattered on Lucy's face, and, without thinking, she raced for the monster on his back, grabbing the cold, skinless body and clinging on. She placed her feet on Sammo's hips, and pulled. The monster tightened its muscles, pressing closer to her friend. Sammo's blood gushed over her.

"Let go of him!" she roared, wrapping her fingers around one of the thin legs and tugging on it. With a soft sucking noise, the limb snapped loose, expelling a gout of foul-smelling discharge. The creature's sac blew up like a balloon, and Lucy took her chance. She punched her fist through, the membrane breaking like fine silk. Purple pus seeped down her arm, making her gag, and she closed her fist around the scrawny mutant within. It vibrated in her hand, releasing a muted cry of pain, and then crunched in her steely grip. At once, the monster's legs loosened. It released Sammo, dropping dead to the ground alongside her.

Sammo fought on, raking his claws down the monster attacking from the front, but he was growing tired. He staggered forwards, one foot catching on a buckled root, and collapsed on top of the creature, crushing it beneath his immense weight. Bones crackled and splintered like burning kindling, and with a loud *pop*, blood and entrails spurted from the ruined carcass.

Click-clack, click-clack.

More were on their way.

Sammo rose, pieces of the flattened monster stuck to his belly, and gathered Lucy up in his paws. She wanted to thank him, but shock was setting in, and as he clattered through the undergrowth, shielding her from harm, Lucy curled into a ball.

She wept as they fled.

What the fuck.

What the actual fuck.

When Sammo came to a stop, he laid Lucy down on the soft ground.

She opened her damp eyes, afraid of what she would find.

The hint of a smile crept onto her lips.

Gone were the dark, skeletal trees, and the webs, and the monsters. Instead, she stared up at an abundance of luscious green foliage and tall, healthy Scots Pine.

Her left hand floated pleasingly in a small loch. She rolled over and crawled to the bank, staring at her reflection. Blood dripped from the tip of her nose and rippled the image, the droplets staining the crystal clear water a dirty red. She splashed the refreshing liquid onto her face, and looked down at her blood-soaked tee-shirt and underpants.

She was lucky to be alive.

Okay, she was missing some skin on her hand, and definitely some hair, and her jeans and jacket were gone forever, but... she was very much alive.

She kicked off her shoes and crawled into the tranquil loch. There, she floated on her back across the surface. The quiet and the colour and the pleasant pine odour helped to relieve the terror that had dragged her to the brink of madness, and she scrubbed at her arms and face in an effort to forget about the scuttling, and—

Stop.

She was safe now, thanks to Sammo. Her friend. Her protector. How was he? She waded to the shore, where he lay on his back, blood pooling around him.

"Sammo!"

God, she hadn't even checked to see if he was okay! Cursing her selfish nature, she splashed out of the loch and ran to him. His wounds were deep, and she figured he needed stitches. But from who? Herself?

Why not? Over the last couple of years she had learnt to sew as a way to extend the lifespan of her clothes, so seriously... why the fuck not? She owed it to Sammo. If she hadn't gone wandering off, he wouldn't have had to rescue her. And anyway, it's not like she could take him to a doctor. They would never understand.

"Can you move?"

His dry tongue lolled out of his mouth, and she dutifully retrieved water from the loch and let him drink from her cupped hands. Then he rose, slowly, to a sitting position. She tried to help, but he must have weighed a ton.

"You've gotta come home with me. Do you understand?" She pointed at him, then at herself. *"Home."*

Sammo's eyes half closed, and he rocked backwards, his head swaying. She grabbed his paw.

"Come on! Snap out of it!"

Wearily, he slumped onto all fours. Lucy patted his head and glanced around. "Ummm... do you know where my home is?"

Sammo groaned and started onwards, and Lucy stayed by his side, stroking his sticky fur as they walked, afraid he would fall on top of her the way he had on that spider... crab... *thing*. Whatever the fuck it was.

Actually, that wasn't a bad name for them.

Whatthefucks.

She smiled to herself as she and Sammo stumbled through the woods, pleased she had lost neither her sense of humour nor her mind.

You almost died today.

"I don't want to think about it."

Sammo gazed up at her.

"Sorry," she said. "Just talking to myself. You'll get used to it. I can't always shut my brain off."

She sang her favourite Smashing Pumpkins songs to offset the gnawing dread in the pit of her stomach. *1979, Cherub Rock, Mayonnaise...* the full repertoire.

It didn't help.

For all she could think about, on that long walk home with her injured friend by her side, were the scarecrows that surrounded her home. They weren't there to frighten off birds, or to protect a field of crops from scavengers.

No, these scarecrows existed for a single nightmarish purpose, one that ran counter to everything Lucy had ever believed in.

They were there to keep the monsters away.

13

———————

Twice, on the way home, Sammo fell to his knees, and twice Lucy coaxed him back up by waving unappetising-looking branches in front of his snout. Like a donkey following a carrot, he trotted on until, at last, they reached the clearing.

The sun hung low, and her dad's van was gone.

Shepherding Sammo into the barn, she closed the double doors and locked them by placing a long plank into the slots. Sammo took four steps, then crumpled into a heap by the generator. Blood matted his fur, staining it a muddy maroon.

"Don't worry, I'll patch you up," she said with unearned confidence. Sure, she could sew a little, enough to raise a hem or fix a pocket, but she had never stitched-up a living creature. Could she give him painkillers? Get him drunk? And would she need to sterilise the needles?

Shit!

She had no idea what she was doing. But Sammo needed her, and Lucy refused to let a lack of knowledge prevent her from trying.

She gathered supplies from the house — her sewing kit, antiseptic cream from the bathroom, tissues, her dad's lighter — and dumped the items in a Sainsbury's carrier bag, before racing back to Sammo, grateful she still had her shoes.

In the barn, she knelt by his side, her fingers shaking as she tried to thread the needle. Sammo uttered a subdued moan as she messed it up for the fifth time.

"I'm sorry." Tears stung her eyes. "I'm trying."

There! The thread was in.

She inspected Sammo's injuries. The savage wounds were equally severe, so she chose one at random and reached delicately for it. His exposed tissue throbbed through the laceration. She gagged, the needle hovering close to his flesh, and tried to push the two edges of skin together.

Wait! She hadn't sterilised the needle yet. Where was the lighter?

An engine rumbled in the distance.

She ran to the barn doors and peered out at her dad's van crunching along the track. Dammit, she had never been so happy to see him. "Wait there," she said to Sammo, and sprinted into the clearing, waving her hands and calling for her dad. He was getting out of the van when he heard her voice, and slammed the door furiously.

"Where the *hell* have you been?" he roared, and Lucy came to a stop. She couldn't recall the last time he had raised his voice at her.

He stormed closer. "I got a call from the school saying you hadn't shown up, and I've spent the whole *fucking day* looking for..."

He trailed off as he neared.

"Lucy!" he cried, and broke into a run. "Oh god! What happened? Who did this to you?"

At first, she was too tired and stressed to understand his reaction. Then she realised she was standing in the field in a blood-soaked tee-shirt and knickers, her bare arms and legs covered in cuts and welts and nasty, purple bruises.

"It's not what you think," she tried to say, but he wasn't listening.

He placed his hands on her shoulders and burst into tears. "Lucy, *who did this to you?"*

She started to explain, then changed her mind.

"It's easier if I show you," she said. "Follow me!"

Her dad took the news surprisingly well.

Lucy supposed finding an injured monster in his barn was preferable to the alternative he had conjured in his mind. She showed him Sammo, and told him she needed his help patching him up, and her dad, to his eternal credit, had shaken his head, rolled up his sleeves, and gotten to work. Though he was no surgeon, he had — as he explained later over a glass of wine — researched how to stitch up a wound for a war novel he had written years ago. He flushed the debris from the wounds with hot water, then sewed them up so that the skin barely touched.

Night had fallen by the time they finished, and they sat with Sammo until her dad made them go inside. There, Lucy showered and dressed in her pyjamas, and tried to eat dinner. The way her dad pushed his oven chips around the plate suggested neither of them were particularly hungry.

She told him about her first meeting with Sammo, and how she had skipped school to see him again, whereupon she had been attacked by an 'animal' in the woods. She didn't go into detail on that — other than making up a lie about getting her jeans and jacket caught on barbed wire during her escape — because she was convinced of two things.

One — that her dad's mind would not be able to handle it. A single monster was enough for him right now, especially as he was still getting over the shock of thinking his daughter had been assaulted.

And most importantly, *two* — that if he understood what horrors lurked within the woods, he would make them leave. Two days earlier, Lucy would have jumped at the idea. But Sammo was injured because of her, and he needed help, and only she — and now her dad — could offer him that.

They couldn't leave him here, not now.

"I really think we should call someone," her dad said, after most of their dinner had ended up in the bin. "An expert, or..."

"No," she said decisively, sitting by the window and gazing out at the barn. "No one else can know."

He took a long sip of wine. "He needs help. More than we can give."

"He'll be okay. We just need to look after him. I'm gonna take tomorrow off school and—"

"Uh-uh, negative," he interrupted. "You're not missing another day of school."

"Dad!"

"I've made my mind up."

She crossed her arms and looked away from him. "I hate you."

"Don't sulk," he said. "I can take care of him."

"I'm not *sulking*."

How could he be so cruel? The idea of being apart from

Sammo was terrible. What if he needed water, or a cuddle? She stared at the barn, wishing she could be with him. "Will you at least pick me up from school?"

"Happily, if it means I know you'll be there. I'll even drive you in." He tried to take another drink, realised his glass was empty, and raised the bottle to his lips. "I was worried sick about you today. When I came home and saw—"

"Okay, dad, I don't want to talk about it." It was bad enough he'd seen her in her underwear. She never wanted to think about it again.

He lit a cigarette, and said, to no one in particular, "There's a *monster* in my barn."

"You should write a story about that," said Lucy, and her dad nodded.

"Maybe I will," he said, and that was how it began.

That night, Lucy alternated between lying in bed and staring out her window. How could she sleep knowing they were out there? Those monsters.

Those whatthefucks.

Each time she laid her head on the pillow and closed her eyes, she visualised that hideous fiend skulking towards her from the shadows. How many were there? And those tunnels... where did they lead? Rab's tale of monsters no longer sounded quite so fanciful. The boy who had lived here, in this very house, had been killed by them. Had he walked into the woods and invited death upon himself?

She would not make that mistake again.

The forest was firmly off-limits. She wouldn't go back in, even with a gun to her head. And once Sammo was at full health, she would tell her dad about the *other* monsters, and they would go home to Edinburgh.

Yeah, that sounded good.

She just needed to look after Sammo for a while.

For what felt like the hundredth time, she got out of bed and leaned her forehead against the window, watching the barn. Was Sammo okay? Was he in pain?

It must be lonely in there, and she wanted to keep him company.

But it was dark outside.

And for all she knew, they were out there, waiting in the shadows.

She climbed into bed and wrapped herself in the duvet.

After today, she wondered if she'd ever sleep again.

14

As promised, Lucy's dad dropped her off at school the next morning. To maintain what little dignity she still possessed, they parked two streets over so no one would see her arrive.

"Swear you'll look after him," she said, as they sat in the van with the engine growling. "Check his injuries. And don't forget his lunch."

"Another mouth to feed," he muttered. "Great."

"He eats leaves and sticks, *Brian*. We can afford those." A grim thought occurred to her. "Oh, but don't go too far into the woods. He, uh, likes the sticks that grow close to the house."

"Don't worry, he's in good hands." He held them up for her to see. "*Healing* hands."

"Who even *are* you?" she asked, then exited the vehicle. "Look after my friend, and stay out of the woods," she reiterated, before slamming the door and walking down the street.

Her dad beeped the horn twice, and she ignored him. When he honked again, she turned and waved with a grimace plastered to her face. Only then did he drive away. "Such a loser," she said, and cut through a lane on her way to school.

God, she hadn't thought of this place at all yesterday.

Did she look presentable? The night before, she had scrubbed the blood and dirt and cobwebs from her face and hair, but she was out of concealer and could do nothing to hide her black eye and the scratches across her cheeks and forehead. But maybe, if her luck was in, nobody would notice?

She saw Rab approaching, and he waved to her. "Awright," he said cheerily, staring at her through his thick glasses. "Fuckin' hell, look at the state of you!"

"Oh, piss off." That was the last thing she needed to hear.

He followed her like a puppy. "Ach, I didnae mean it like that. Whit happened? You fall oot ae a tree?"

"Yes, actually. Thanks to your sister."

"She pushed ya?" He wrinkled his nose. "What were you and ma sister doin' up a tree?"

"She didn't *push* me, she... it doesn't matter. I'm here now."

"Cool." He smiled at her. "I'll walk you tae class."

She had little choice, so Rab accompanied her to morning registration, chatting animatedly about how the second Jurassic Park was coming out next year, and asking if she'd seen part one. She had, but there were more important matters to discuss.

"Hey, remember you were telling me about those monsters?" she asked, trying to sound casual.

"What, they yins that ate Bobby Chow?"

"Yeah. Those ones."

"What about 'em?"

She shrugged nonchalantly. "What do you know about them?"

"Everything."

"Really?" She gripped his arm without realising. "What are they?"

"Well, ah dinnae ken *that*."

"Okay. Well, how many are there?"

"How would ah ken?"

"Because you just said..." She paused, rubbing her eyes. This was somehow going worse than expected. "Can you tell me *anything* useful?"

"I thought you didnae believe in monsters."

"Well—"

"You called me a wee prick."

"I did, and I'm sorry. But I need to—"

"Aw, hang on!" Rab's jaw dropped. "You've seen 'em, haven't you?"

"What? Of course not."

"Have too. Aye, you've proper seen one, like!"

"I haven't," she hissed.

"Makes sense," he said. "What with you livin' in Bobby Chow's house and aw."

"I haven't seen any fucking monsters!" she shouted. A few pupils nearby glanced over at her, and she lowered her voice. "So stop asking."

Rab stared at her, stealing a furtive glance at her chest. "Aye, awright. Guess you wouldnae be here if you'd seen them. You'd be..." — he slid a finger across his neck, then added, somewhat unnecessarily — "...pure dead an' that. They dinnae let anyone live."

"But what if there were good monsters too?"

"Whit, in the woods?" Rab chuckled. "You've changed your fuckin' tune! The other day, you were all like, *shut up*

Rab, you speccy cunt, and now yer aw, *tell me about the monsters, Rab! I need to know!*"

God, he was loud, but Lucy couldn't help laughing. "Yeah, that is *exactly* what I said. Great impression, by the way. Really captured my essence."

"We've aw got our wee skills," he grinned, and looked shyly at the floor. "That's your classroom. Wanna meet at the wall for lunch, aye?"

"Yeah," she said, and smiled back at him. "I'd like that."

As they ate together on the playground wall, Lucy learned little of the monsters other than some old myth about Helsbridge being built on the literal bridge to hell, but one nugget of information set her mind racing.

Rab told her the legend of a mysterious warrior — The Guardian of the Forest — who patrolled the boundary between our world and hell, and kept the monsters from crossing over. Rab had made fun of that part, but Lucy's thoughts had turned immediately to Sammo. Okay, so he didn't exactly *look* like a Guardian of the Forest. But who said warriors couldn't be hairy vegetarian monsters?

She refused Rab's offer to recount the grisly details of each slain child, so they ate lunch and chatted about normal stuff. It turned out Rab was seventeen, and he showed her his attempt at a moustache to prove it. They spoke about movies and music, and he revealed that the Nirvana patch on Isobel's jacket was actually his, and that she had stolen it because she liked the smiley face logo. She knew nothing of their music, which annoyed Rab, because they were his favourite band. This prompted a good-natured argument over who was better; Pearl Jam or Nirvana.

When the bell rang, Lucy was disappointed their discussion had to end, though she was confident she'd won the argument. They agreed to meet in the same spot the next day, and said their goodbyes.

As Rab walked across the playground, he glanced over his shoulder at her. They made fleeting eye contact, and Lucy turned away, embarrassed to be caught looking. She had spent much of the conversation desperate to tell him about Sammo, partly because she wanted to share her secret with someone other than her dad, but also because she felt the need to impress the boy. Should she invite him round?

Her cheeks flushed, and she kept her head down and scurried to class, a double period of art with Miss Wade, where she spent the entire lesson thinking of how best to ask Rab if he wanted to hang out without sounding needy or desperate.

She was still debating her course of action when the final bell rang. School was over, and her dad would be waiting to pick up her up. Chucking her art supplies in her plastic bag — she really needed to get a replacement schoolbag — she rushed to the door in an attempt to be first out.

"Lucy, can you wait behind?" called Miss Wade.

What the hell?

"Ooooooh," said a couple of her classmates, as if she was in big trouble. She waited by Miss Wade's desk as the pupils filed out of the classroom.

"How are you?" the teacher asked once they were alone.

She looked at the clock. "I'm fine."

"That's good. Finding your way around okay?"

"Yup. Everything is fine." She didn't mean to be abrupt, but her dad was waiting, and Sammo—

"You don't look fine, if you don't mind me saying."

Lucy turned to her. "Huh?"

"Your eye. Those cuts. Did someone... do that to you?"

"No. I fell."

"You fell?"

"Out of a tree."

"A *tree?*"

"That's right. I climbed a tree, and fell out of it. I'm okay, though. Never better."

She danced an awkward shuffle to prove her point, then instantly regretted it.

Miss Wade nodded slowly. "You know I'm here for you if you ever need to talk, right?" She offered a sincere smile. "From one new girl to another."

"I know," said Lucy. "But I'm okay, honestly."

"Life can be hard without someone to talk to."

"Tell me about it. I'm sixteen years old. I know how hard life can be."

"I'm sure you do."

Lucy glanced at the window. "Can I go now? My dad's picking me up, and he's, uh, a busy man."

"Oh yeah? What does your dad do?"

Enough with the questions!

"He's an author."

Come on, come on! Sammo's waiting!

"Oh, an author? How exciting! What's his name? Maybe I've read something of his."

"Brian Brannigan. He used to be famous, but not any—"

"Brian Brannigan?" Miss Wade's eyes widened. "*The* Brian Brannigan?"

Lucy shrugged. "I don't know if he's *the* Brian Brannigan. He's definitely *a* Brian Brannigan."

"The writer of *Flight of the Goose?* And *Five Days to Hell?*"

"Yeah, that's my dad."

The teacher's mouth opened, but no words came out.

"Do you... like his books?" asked Lucy.

"Like? I mean, that's an understatement. *Death of a Soldier* changed my *life.*"

"Cool. I've never met a fan before." She bit her lip. "So... may I go?"

"What? Yeah, of course. And say hi to your dad for me. No, wait, don't do that, he'll think I'm crazy. God, he probably gets this all the time. Tell him... tell him I'm a big fan. No, a huge fan. His number one fan. Is that too much?"

"I'll tell him something."

"*The Brian Brannigan,*" Miss Wade muttered, as Lucy hurried from the classroom, waiting until she was out of sight before pulling a face.

"That was weird," she said, before racing down the stairs and out of the school building. She nipped down the lane and threw herself into the van beside her father.

"Good day at—"

"Drive, Brian!" she shouted, and drive he did.

15

———————

Sammo's condition had improved dramatically.

The monster raised his round head when Lucy entered the barn, and she ran and hugged him.

"I cleaned and dressed his wounds," her dad said, as he shut the barn door. "I almost didn't have to. They're healing fast. Faster than I thought possible."

"Is that right, Sammo?" asked Lucy. He licked her face.

"Sure is," her dad said. "I've never seen anything like it. Must have had a pretty talented surgeon."

She ignored him, her attention focused on Sammo. "Can I get you something to eat?" Her dad had piled a large stack of branches and twigs beneath the farming tools on the wall. She retrieved one, and held it to Sammo's mouth while he chewed on the leaves.

"Sorry you had to look after him all day," said Lucy. She kissed Sammo's fuzzy neck. "I can stay off tomorrow and—"

"Lucy, we've been over this. No more skipping school. After Friday, you've got all summer to lounge around. And anyway, I don't mind. He kinda gave me the idea for a new book."

"Oh yeah? About what?"

"About him, you dope."

Lucy turned to her father. "What? That was my idea! I told you to write a story about him!"

"When?"

"Yesterday!" she cried.

"Really? I don't remember."

"Hmmmm." She leaned against Sammo. "So what's it about, this book of yours?"

"What do you think? It's about a man who finds a monster and nurses him back to health. It's all a metaphor, of course, for—"

"Wait, did you say a *man* finds him?"

"You've got good ears."

"Don't change the subject, Brian. You can't make the story about a man. *I* was the one who found him. He's my friend, not yours!"

"That may be, but no one wants to read a story about a teenager. They're not interesting. No offence, but adults make for much more compelling protagonists."

Lucy glared at him, half-teasing and half-miffed. "You think I'm not compelling?"

"I didn't say *you*. But yeah, I'd say ninety-nine percent of adults are more interesting than ninety-nine percent of teenagers. It's just a fact. We've lived longer, so we have more life experience to draw on."

"Uh-huh. And this *man* in your book. Does he have a daughter?"

"I've not decided yet." He was suppressing a grin, and she knew a joke was incoming. "Might give him a son."

She refused to acknowledge the comment, and turned away as her dad giggled to himself. It was what her mum called his *secret laugh,* and she hadn't heard it for a while. Lucy smiled, and held Sammo.

His whiskers twitched.

"Hey," said Lucy. "That tickles!"

Sammo sat bolt upright and turned towards the door.

"He hears something," her dad said.

Lucy's blood ran cold. The monsters. What else could it be? Warily, she eyed the pitchfork and the axe on the wall, her heart rate increasing exponentially. "Dad, there's something I haven't told—"

"It's a car," he said.

"What? Oh…" She heard it too, and relaxed, the tension leaving her rigid body. She had almost blurted out… wait, shit, a car? That wasn't much better! No one could know about Sammo.

"Are you expecting someone?" she asked.

"No. The only person I've told about this place is my agent, and he lives in London. Also, he doesn't really talk to me since I stopped making him money." He motioned to her. "Come on, let's see who it is. Might just be the postie."

Lucy raised her index finger at Sammo. "Stay," she commanded, and then she and her father left the barn and shut the door firmly.

A dark green car was pulling up in front of their house.

It's the authorities, Lucy panicked. *They've come to take Sammo away.*

In a Mini Cooper? Unlikely.

The door to the Mini opened. Lucy watched as Miss Wade got out in the same paint-splattered jeans and cardigan she had worn in school.

"Shit," she said to her father. "It's my art teacher."

"What the hell does she want?"

Miss Wade hadn't spotted them yet. She was too busy staring in confused horror at the scarecrows.

"Don't mind them," Lucy shouted, jogging towards her teacher. She needed to intercept Miss Wade before she got too close to the barn. "They were here when we moved in."

"Hi, Lucy," Miss Wade said with a wave, then strode right past her. "Mr Brannigan, I presume?"

"That's me."

"Hi. I'm Elli Wade, Lucy's art teacher."

Lucy grinned. Not only had Miss Wade brushed her hair, but she was wearing lippy.

Her dad extended his hand. "Pleased to meet you, Elli. I'm Brian."

"She *kno-o-o-ows,*" said Lucy, stretching the last syllable out like elastic. "I forgot to tell you, Miss Wade says she's your *number one fan.*"

"Lucy!" snapped Miss Wade, her cheeks reddening. "I'm sorry, Mr Brannigan. Your daughter happened to mention that you were her father, and then *I* happened to mention that I'd read one of your books, and—"

"You've read more than one," said Lucy, enjoying her newfound ability to make her teacher squirm.

"Okay, yes, I have. But—"

"And you said *Flight of the Goose* changed your life."

"That is *not* true," said Miss Wade, before quietly adding, "It was *Death of a Soldier.* But that's not why I'm here. Mr Brannigan—"

"Please, call me Brian." His voice sounded unfamiliar to Lucy's ears. Treacly, almost.

"Okay, Brian," her teacher said with a smile. "I was wondering if—"

A loud snore from the barn silenced her. All three of them turned their heads.

"What was that?" Miss Wade asked.

"What was what?" replied Lucy. "I didn't hear anything. Did you hear anything, dad?"

"Not a thing."

A moment's silence, broken by another phlegmy rumble.

"Oh, *that,*" said Lucy. "That's Sammo. He's... our horse."

Miss Wade brightened. "You have a horse? How wonderful! Can I see?"

"No," said Lucy. "He's sleeping."

"But can't I just—"

"You should never wake a sleeping horse," her dad said.

"It's bad luck," Lucy added. "Seven years, I think."

Miss Wade stared at the barn. "Really? I've never heard that one before."

"Sure you have," said Lucy. "It's an old saying. Let sleeping horses lie."

"I think that's dogs."

"That's what the dogs want you to believe."

Lucy stared at her teacher, unsure what to say next.

Luckily, her dad piped up. "What can I do for you, Elli? I'm sure you didn't come here to discuss aphorisms."

Distracted, Miss Wade said, "Actually, I was hoping to talk to you in private, Brian."

"What about?"

Lucy rolled her eyes. "If she tells you in front of me, it wouldn't exactly be private, would it?" She turned to Miss Wade. "Sorry, my dad's not very good with words. Believe it or not, I actually write all his books for him."

Miss Wade laughed at that, and Lucy swelled with pride the way she always did when she managed to make an adult laugh.

In the barn, Sammo sneezed, followed by a long, flatulent parp.

"Is your horse okay?" asked Miss Wade. "Should we check on him?"

"He's fine," said Lucy. "Under the weather, that's all. Now, why don't you two go inside for your private chat, and I'll give Sammo his, umm, medicine?"

"Great idea," said her dad, his voice booming across the clearing as he escorted Miss Wade towards the house. "I'll make us both a coffee."

"Thank you," Miss Wade said, glancing one more time at the barn. Lucy grinned and waved goodbye to her. She must have looked like a maniac, because her teacher turned away.

Job done.

She returned to the barn to wait with Sammo, expecting to hear her teacher driving away shortly. But when she checked an hour later, desperate for a pee, Miss Wade's car was still parked outside. Refusing to be held hostage in the barn, she stalked across the field and into the house. There, she found the pair laughing together in the living room like old pals.

Miss Wade was the first to notice her.

"Lucy," she said, checking her watch. "Sorry, we lost track of time. We started talking about Brian's... I mean, your father's books, and, well... I do apologise."

"That's okay. I hadn't realised this was a social call."

Her dad cleared his throat. Had he changed into a different shirt? "Sit down, Luce. Miss Wade has been telling me—"

"Can I pee first?"

"Of course," he said. "Be my guest."

"It's my house too, Brian," she called, as she ran up the stairs to use her dad's en-suite. There was no way she was peeing in the room next to her art teacher. When she finished, she came downstairs to find her dad seeing Miss Wade off in the hallway.

"It was a pleasure to meet you," he was saying, in a deeper-than-usual voice that made Lucy's toes curl. "And don't worry about Lucy. Kids get bumps and scrapes all the time. She's always been the adventurous, nature-loving type. I think she takes it from me."

She almost gasped, and stomped her feet down the hallway to let him know she could hear his lies.

Surprised, he turned to her. "Now, uh, remember what I said, Lucy. No more climbing trees, you hear me?"

"There goes my summer," she deadpanned.

He glared at her, then affixed a smile to his lips before turning back to Miss Wade. "Have a safe trip home."

"I will. See you in school, Lucy." Miss Wade hesitated in the doorway, nodded, then left.

Her dad closed the door.

"You okay, Mr Nature-lover?" asked Lucy.

"Hmm? Yeah, absolutely." He chuckled to himself. "You know, it's amazing the kids in your class get any work done at all. The teachers did not look like that in my day."

It was true, she supposed. Miss Wade was very pretty, and unlike most people under sixty, she had actually read and enjoyed her dad's books.

"Do you... *like* her?" she prodded.

"What? No! Not like *that,* if that's what you mean." He glanced out the window. "*Is* that what you mean?"

"Oh my god," she muttered. "If you fancy her, just ask her out."

"You're crazy," he said, and walked away, shaking his head like a proper disapproving dad.

An engine spluttered into life outside, and a tingle of mischief worked its way from Lucy's gut to her brain.

She ran for the door.

"Where are you going?" her dad shouted.

"She forgot her purse," Lucy called back, as she burst through the front door into the clearing. "Wait there!"

Miss Wade's Mini was halfway up the track. In a matter of seconds, it would trundle round the first bend and vanish from sight.

"Wait!" Lucy called, waving her arms and giving chase. "Come back!"

The Mini slowed, and Miss Wade wound down the window as Lucy ran towards her. Jesus, was she going to spend the whole summer running?

"Everything okay?" Miss Wade asked.

Lucy caught up to her and rested her hands on the window frame, almost out of breath. "Yeah," she panted, and leaned in closer. "Miss Wade, there's something my dad wanted to ask you."

"So what was all that about?" her dad asked, as she traipsed inside and collapsed onto the living room easy chair.

"What do you mean?" she replied innocently.

"You know damn well what I mean." He narrowed his eyes. "I'm talking about a few minutes ago, when you went tearing off out the house like a blue-arsed flea. And don't give me that line about forgetting her purse, because you had *nothing* in your hands."

"Oh, calm down, dad. I asked Miss Wade if she wanted you to sign her books, that's all."

"Aye?"

"Yup. She's got them all, you know."

"Is that so?"

"Mmm-hmm."

"A woman of impeccable taste," he said admiringly.

Lucy picked up an out-of-date copy of *Woman's Weekly.* "If you say so." She flicked through the pages. "Jeez, someone's already finished the crossword." Aware of her dad's lingering presence, she kept leafing through the magazine. "Want me to read your horoscope?"

"Lucy," he said.

"Yes?"

He took a seat opposite her. "Did she want her books signed or not?"

"Oh, yeah, sorry, I forgot what we were talking about." She laid the magazine aside and put her dad out of his misery. "She said she'd like that very much."

"Okay then." He pursed his lips. "No problemo."

"I thought you'd say that. Well, maybe not *no problemo,* but something equally dorky." Then, as if it were nothing, she added, "So I invited her round for dinner on Friday."

"You *what?*"

"By the way, I told her I was asking on your behalf, so play along, okay?"

He left his seat and paced across the room. "That's... look, you can't go around asking your teachers out on dates for me, Lucy. You may be my daughter, but this time you've gone too far." He paused by the window as if trying to catch one more glimpse of Miss Wade. "So what did she say?"

"She said that sounded lovely."

"Lucy!"

"I'm sorry, but watching you flirt was too painful. I thought I'd cut to the chase."

"I could have asked her myself. If I'd wanted to, that is."

"Don't you want to?"

He stared out at the forest. Rain drummed against the window pane. "That's beside the point."

"Well, you can call the school tomorrow and cancel, if you like. But she seemed very excited, and you don't want to disappoint your only fan, do you?"

"My only... wait, *what?*"

She stood and stretched. "Come on, dad. I'll make dinner, and you can start thinking about what you're going to wear on your big date." With the *coup de grâce* delivered, she wandered smugly into the kitchen and rummaged through the cupboards for inspiration. She pulled a tin of beans from the shelf and brushed a cobweb from the top, and for the first time that afternoon, her thoughts turned to the lurking horrors within the forest.

She knew she should tell her dad about them. And she would, when the time was right. But not now. Not when things were looking up. She had made two friends, and now her dad had a date with her cool art teacher. The more she considered it, the more their fortunes seemed to be improving. She just hoped life could stay like this... for a while, at least.

For surely even a little happiness was preferable to none at all?

16

In a small farmhouse on the edge of Helsbridge, Margot McFarlane glanced at the kitchen clock in dismay.

Ten to eight.

Nearly bedtime.

She stacked the last dish on the drying rack, and muttered, "Fuck's sake."

What would her old mates back in Dundee think of her going to bed before nine wearing a sensible knee-length cotton nightie and tartan slippers? A few years ago, Margot and the gang wouldn't even *start* drinking until after eight, getting progressively drunker and sharing ribald tales of awful men and bad shags, before hitting the bars and clubs in risqué outfits that left nothing to the imagination. There, they would party the night away, indulging in drink, drugs, and sex until the sun rose, before making the walk of shame home, tugging their skirts down over their arse cheeks and clutching their heels in their hands.

God, she missed those days.

Sure, the office job had been boring, but the weekends — oh, those wild weekends! — more than made up for that.

Then she had met Alf.

Her friends had laughed when she told them she was in love with a farmer, especially one with a teenage son from a previous marriage. But the whirlwind romance soon led to an engagement, and then to their wedding day, and, finally, to this. Now, instead of dolling herself up in makeup and skimpy dresses, she wore welly boots and overalls and waded through cow shit. And rather than stumbling home at sunrise, she had to be in bed by nine, because life on the farm began at four every morning.

"You signed up for this," she said, staring out the window at the setting sun and wondering what her old gang — Betty and Carly and Big Stacey — were up to right now. Probably cracking open the first bottle of bubbly. No, wait, it was Thursday. How silly of her.

They'd be on the vodka.

Vodka Thursdays, they had called them. It wasn't a clever name, but it didn't need to be, because they were downing shots of vodka on a Thursday night. Those Fridays in the office were a total write-off.

Margot smiled at the memory. Vodka Thursdays. Sambuca Saturdays. The dreaded Buckfast Tuesdays. Had they all been alcoholics? Possibly, though it hadn't felt that way at the time.

God, she fancied a drink.

Alf was out working the fields in his tractor. She waved to him through the window, but he didn't notice. Had he forgotten his glasses? Despite his insistence that his vision was flawless, he had promised he would wear them. How often did she have to remind the big galoot? Sometimes, between her husband and Phil, it felt like she was the mother of *two* children.

Upstairs, Phil stomped around his room, the football

blaring from his telly. How one skinny little boy could make so much racket, she'd never know.

She opened the drinks cabinet and unscrewed the cap of Alf's rum. The alcohol tasted good, and it would help her sleep. She took another swig. Over the noise of the football, she heard Phil shouting.

Phil.

What a ridiculous thing to call a teenager. When he was older, it might suit him, but Phil wasn't a young person's name. It was the name of a used car salesman, or a stand-up comedian, and her layabout stepson was neither.

A colossal bang from upstairs rattled the light fixture.

"Phil!" screamed Margot. "Keep it down!"

The ceiling groaned. It sounded like the wee shite was rolling across the floorboards.

"Right, that's it!" she shouted. "If you've got a girl up there, she'd better have her knickers on and be out the window by the time I climb the stairs!"

Was this what her life had become? Telling-off teenagers for doing exactly what she had done at their age? She was such a hypocrite. But anything to ruin Phil's grotty little fun was worth doing. After all, she was the one who had to load his stained, crispy boxer shorts into the washing machine every week.

Psyching herself up for an argument, she tucked the rum safely into the cabinet and stormed out of the kitchen, listening to Phil's muffled grunts as she climbed the stairs. With the sweet taste of alcohol coating her mouth, she was abso-bloody-lutely ready to tear a strip off the wee ratbag right in front of whichever daft tart he'd dragged back to his filthy lair.

A loud bang stopped her in her tracks, followed by the shattering of glass. The roar of the football crowd abruptly silenced. Christ, they were fair going at it. Well, if that was his TV, he could save up his own money to replace it. The obnoxious little shit needed to learn the value of—

"*Aaaaargh!*"

Margot's blood hardened in her veins.

Phil's scream was not one of pleasure.

She gripped the bannister. Like everyone in Helsbridge, she had heard the stories. Alf had broken the news to her one quiet evening over supper, two weeks after they had married and moved in to his farmhouse.

That bastard.

Had she known earlier, she never would have agreed to live here. Not in a place infested with monsters. But it couldn't be them in Phil's room. Not here, not now. Everyone knew the monsters stayed within their boundary.

A new sound bled from behind the bedroom door.

Thick, juicy slurping.

It either meant Phil was a more considerate lover than she had given him credit for, or—

No.

Impossible.

Cautiously, she resumed her climb. A step creaked underfoot, and the slurping stopped.

"Phil? Is that you?"

A bloodcurdling scream erupted from inside the bedroom, and that was all Margot needed to hear. She turned and started down the stairs. Alf kept a farming shotgun in—

The bedroom door flew open and crashed against the wall.

Click-clack, click-clack.

Margot screamed and kept running. Above her, the

monster — for what else could it be? — scurried across the hallway, its legs clicking maddeningly on the floorboards.

How could it make it this far from the woods?

She reached the bottom of the stairs and skidded on the rug, slamming into the door. Her sweaty hands fumbled for the handle.

Click-clack, click-clack, down the stairs it came.

Part of her wanted to turn around, to put an image to the folk tales and horror stories. She had *heard* about the monsters, but no one could ever describe what they looked like.

Only the sounds they made. The clicking, and the screams.

They had all heard the screams.

The lure was what the old-timers called it.

Aye, I heard the lure last night, they would say to each other. *They're getting hungry again.*

But they *never* left the woods. Something was wrong.

The balance had shifted.

Margot hurtled through the door and closed it, ensuring the lock caught. As she did, the creature on the other side slammed into it. The wood bulged, but did not break.

Kicking off her slippers, she ran. Alf's tractor was two fields over.

She had to reach it.

"Alf!" she screamed.

The monster pounded against the front door. Her stupid nightie prevented her from running, so she lifted the hem to her waist and bunched it in her fist.

"Alf, help!"

Stones and rocks stabbed into her soles, and she stumbled on the uneven, recently ploughed ground, desperately trying to keep her balance as she approached the first of the two barbed wire fences.

Placing her hands on the wooden post, she jumped, throwing her legs over in an ungainly fashion. Her trailing nightie snagged on the jagged wire and tore, splitting up the seam, but she somehow stuck the landing.

Only then did she notice the silence.

The monster no longer battered the door. All was still, save for the grumble of the tractor's engine in the adjacent field. Warily, Margot glanced around at the shadows.

Where was it?

A window in the farmhouse smashed, and something heavy landed on the dirt.

Click-clack, click-clack.

Good god, it was out.

Margot ran.

"Alf!" Her throat was raw, but the tractor trundled on. She waved both hands above her head. Could he not see her white nightgown?

The creature was close, but there was only one fence between her and her husband. She could make it.

She would have to.

Almost there.

Her foot slipped in the mud, and her poor heart stopped beating.

"No fucking way," she snarled, pushing up from the ground with her fingertips and righting herself.

She reached the fence, and, just as she had done the first time, used the post to vault the barbed wire. Too late, she realised the near-fall had robbed her of momentum.

Her leg slipped between the taut wires. The rusted spikes scored deep grooves down her leg, and she toppled forwards, the barbed wire digging in and tightening around her thigh. Margot screamed as she hung upside down, the razor-sharp metal penetrating her flesh. She tried to wrench the limb free, but as she pulled, the knotted metal only dug deeper into her soft, bloody muscle, spilling blood down her leg.

Click-clack, click-clack.

Strung up like a carcass in a butcher shop window, Margot's own mutilated body blocked much of her view of the monster. She saw its hideous legs marching towards her, and a vague pink glow that lit up the surrounding area.

"Fuck off!" she roared, and in a final outburst of deranged energy, she yanked her leg free, screaming in agony as she did so. Rivers of dark blood gushed from the rents in her mangled limb as it thumped uselessly onto the ground in a quivering mess of tattered skin and ruptured nerves.

"Alf!" she choked, digging her fingers into the dirt and hauling herself away from the fence. The tractor was coming towards her. Surely he would see her now!

Two sharp blades closed around her ankle. She looked over her shoulder at the fleshy pincer splitting her skin, and before she could do anything, the claw snapped shut, severing her foot. Margot vomited as the ragged stump spurted blood. The monster moved closer, looming over her. Claws tore through her flimsy nightgown, shredding it, and she rolled onto her back.

"Get away from me!" She punched the dark shape with both hands. "Get the fuck away!"

The monster caught one fist in its claw. White hot pain flared through Margot's hand as three fingers and a thumb dropped onto her chest in a wave of hot blood.

It was all too much. With the spectre of death rapidly approaching, she let her head slump back onto the dirt.

From there, she saw Alf's tractor passing, the heavy work vehicle only fifteen feet from her prone body and the beast that cruelly ravaged it.

And as Margot McFarlane's eyes closed, and her life ebbed away, she looked directly at her husband, his hands gripping the wheel, utterly oblivious to all around him.

"You bastard," she growled, her body jerking as the monster shredded her stomach.

How many times did she have to tell him to wear his fucking glasses?

PART II

17

———

It was Friday, and the school crackled with anticipation. All that stood between the pupils and the summer holidays was one half-day of learning, though for Lucy, the more pressing concern was her dad's impending date with Miss Wade. The day before, they had driven to Auchenmullan to get some groceries from the local Spar so Lucy could prepare the dinner. She had settled on a chicken pasta and bruschetta, which she had learned to make in her Home Economics class.

They also picked up fresh bandages and medical supplies for Sammo, not that he needed them. He was recuperating well. *Miraculously well,* was how her dad had described his recovery. The scars had almost entirely healed, and his fur was growing back. Lucy thought Sammo was well enough to return to his nest, but he seemed to enjoy the pampering, and she was happy for him to stay as long as he liked.

And so there she sat, in morning registration, juggling thoughts of Sammo and her dad and pasta dinners, when a squeal of feedback assaulted her ears.

The classroom silenced. No one knew what was happening.

The ear-piercing shriek abated, and a tiny speaker crackled in the corner of the room.

"Pupils," said a garbled voice. *"This is Mrs Dalry, your headteacher."*

Lucy wondered if this system had ever been used before. She doubted it, judging by the plume of dust emerging from the small speaker as it vibrated.

"I'm afraid," Mrs Dalry said, *"I have some upsetting news to relay. One of your classmates, Philip McFarlane, has been murdered."*

One girl gasped. Another burst into tears.

"Ah fuckin' telt ye," someone whispered.

Mrs Dalry continued in her stern, no-nonsense tone. *"Therefore, until further notice, all residents of Kingussie and the surrounding towns must adhere to a strict curfew. No-one under eighteen may be out after six pm, and everyone must remain indoors after nine, unless special permission is granted by the local constabulary."*

"Aye, fuck that for a laugh," muttered a boy.

"I'm sure you will all join me in sending good wishes to Phil McFarlane's father, who lost both his son and his wife in the attack. And may I remind all pupils that Fiona Cooper has been missing for several days now, and anyone with information as to her whereabouts is urged to come forwards. Let us now bow our heads in prayer."

Lucy bowed her head, partly out of respect, but mostly from shock.

Two people dead?

Killed?

And a girl missing?

She wanted more information. Where did the McFarlanes live? And had they been murdered by a human, or by something... else?

She needed answers, dammit, and she had a good idea where to find them.

Come lunchtime, Rab was waiting for her at the wall with his hand lost in a seemingly bottomless packet of Golden Wonder crisps.

"Take it you heard," he said, as she clambered up beside him.

"About the boy?"

"Obviously," said Rab. "It's aw anyone's talking about."

"Did you know him?"

"Naw, no really. He was in your year. I knew his cousin Gary, though. Right wee cunt. Phil seemed awright. Rubbish name, though, eh? Phil McFarlane. More like Phil McCrack-en!" He elbowed her. "Get it? Fill-ma-crack-in!"

"Yeah, I got it." She took a bite of her sandwich and waited for Rab to stop laughing. "So what happened?"

"What, wi Phil?" His face turned serious. "Monsters got 'im. And his ma. Fuckin' bloodbath, like. His dad found them. She was spread out along the field, and Phil was in his bedroom. Or what wis left of 'im."

Lucy shivered. "How do you know all this?"

"Cos I'm nosy as fuck."

"No shit."

"And Isobel's going oot wi' a police cadet fae Auchen-mullan, and she gets aw the goss fae him."

"And she tells *you*?"

Rab laughed at that. He laughed more than anyone she had ever met. "Naw. But we've got two phones in our hoose, so I listen in on her calls. She's babysitting at the Richard-sons on Saturday, and she's invited him roond. Says she wants to lose her vir—"

"Focus, Rab. I need to know about the murders. Where did Phil live?"

He looked thoughtful. "Outside Helsbridge. No that far fae you, actually. You should move."

"I can't," she said. "Not yet."

"Why no?"

She gazed across the empty playground. She *wanted* to tell him about Sammo. But could she trust him?

"Here, I made you something," he said, dipping his hand into his schoolbag and pulling out a cassette. "Just some songs I thought you might like. If you dinnae want it, that's fine. I wis bored last night, that's aw."

She took the C90 tape from him. According to the hand-written track listing, the first song was *Burn* by The Cure, from the *Crow* soundtrack. Good choice. Next up was Foo Fighters, followed by Faith No More and a band she'd never heard of called Baby Chaos.

"Thank you," she said, and blushed. "That's really kind of you."

He pulled a face and looked away. "Whatever." Then, quieter, he added, "It's ma favourite songs."

"I'll listen tonight. Then maybe I'll make you one." She nudged him with her shoulder. "If you're lucky."

"That'd be cool."

"Hey, why don't you come to my house tomorrow after-noon?" She couldn't believe the words were tumbling out of her mouth. "We could listen to our tapes together."

"Aye?"

"Sure."

"Awright then. I'll cycle roond after lunch."

"Perfect," said Lucy.

"But you go straight home fae school, and stay inside the night."

"You sound like a teacher."

"Aye," said Rab. "Maybe. But ma folks are sayin' that something's wrong. The monsters dinnae normally leave the forest. Whatever used tae stop them comin'... it's no there anymore. And I like you, Lucy." He offered her a sad smile. "I dinnae want to come round tomorrow and find you... y'know."

"You won't," she said. "I've got protection."

"Oh aye? A fuckin' machine gun?"

"No, better than that. Remember you asked if I'd seen a monster? Well, I have." She leaned in close — but not too close, she hoped — and whispered, "I have one in my barn."

"The fuck you do."

"Honestly!"

"Is it deid?"

"Dead? No! He's my friend. He's one of the good monsters. He saved me from the bad ones. Twice." She kicked her heels against the wall. "I call him Sammo."

Rab regarded her quizzically. "Bollocks. There are nae guid monsters."

"Okay," said Lucy. "Well, you can tell him that when you meet him." And with that, she jumped down and started walking to class. Her heart beat madly. Was she really going to share her special secret with someone? And more importantly... had she just asked a boy out?

18

———

Lucy set the ingredients for dinner on the kitchen counter and consulted her handwritten recipe. Sauce stains dotted the paper, and she eyed the cook-books on the shelf above her. It was too late to use them, but she would remember in future. Who knows, one day she might even convince her dad to try his hand at cooking?

She listened to his footsteps as he paced back and forth above her. For over an hour, he had been pottering about and trying on various outfits. It was highly unusual behaviour for a man who never put more than thirty seconds' thought into what he wore.

"I don't have to dress well," he once told her. *"I'm a writer, not a gigolo."* She hadn't known what the word meant, but when she looked it up, she had giggled for the rest of the day.

She opened the dried pasta and checked the clock. Miss Wade was due to arrive in half an hour. Her dad should be ready by now.

"Fine," she muttered, and left the kitchen, rolling her

eyes. "Dinner can wait." Upstairs, she knocked softly on his bedroom door. "Everything okay in there?"

After an uncomfortably long pause, he said, "Uh, yeah."

"That doesn't sound very convincing. Are you dressed? I'm coming in."

"Go for it."

She opened the door and found him fussing with a red tie in front of the mirror. His creased pink shirt was tucked into navy trousers, and pale green socks adorned his feet.

"Dad, what the fuck are you wearing?"

He looked alarmed. "Is it not right?"

"You look like a rainbow."

"Too many colours?"

"Doesn't exactly scream hot date."

"It's not a date, Lucy." He yanked the tie from under his collar. "It's just dinner."

She sniffed the air. "Then why do I smell your expensive aftershave?"

"Jesus, you're like a bloodhound." He tossed the tie on the bed and sat heavily beside it. "Lucy, I have no idea what I'm doing."

"I can see that. Here, let me help." She searched inside his closet. "First of all, you don't want to look too formal. You're a man of leisure, so no shirts tucked in, and *no* handkerchiefs."

"What if I need to blow my nose?"

"Then go to the bathroom like a normal person."

"Normal is—"

"I know, dad. Overrated." She put her hands on her hips. "But an ironed hankie isn't the cool kinda weird, is it? You want to wear something casual. Do you own any fun clothes?"

"What about my Hawaiian shirt? That's wacky."

"On second thoughts, don't talk. What about this?" She pulled out a plain white tee and tossed it at him. "The trousers are fine, but lose the socks. Swap them for black ones. Now, what are we going to do with your hair?"

"Nothing. It looks smart."

"A side parting? You look like Hitler." She examined his hair, shaking her head so he could see her disappointment. "Wait there," she said, then ran through to her room, returning with a can of hairspray.

"What the hell are you doing?" her dad asked, leaning away from her.

"I'm just going to muss it up a little." She ruffled his hair, and fixed it with copious amounts of hairspray. "There, much better. Don't touch it!" She gazed at his forlorn expression. "What's wrong now?"

"I'm thinking I should cancel."

"What? Why? I just did your hair!"

Angrily, he ran his hands through it. "This isn't me, okay? I don't use hairspray, I don't have fun clothes, and I definitely don't go on dates. I've not been on one for... I dunno, twenty years or something."

He was stressing, and she perched next to him on the bed. "You'll be great. You look very handsome."

"No. I'm going to cancel."

"Fine. You have her phone number?"

"*Fuck.* Okay, when she arrives, answer the door and tell her I'm sick. Tell her I'm dead."

"Don't you like Miss Wade?"

"Yeah, but... it doesn't feel right."

"Because of mum?" She took his hand. "She'd want you to move on."

"You don't know that," he said quietly.

"Of course I do. It's been two years, dad. I know you miss

her. I do too, and not just sometimes. Literally *every single day*. But no one's asking you to forget about her, or replace her." A tear ran down her cheek. "All I'm saying is, wouldn't it be nice to have someone to talk to other than me? I mean, I know I'm super smart, and very funny... but isn't it time you met someone?"

"Maybe," he sighed.

"That's not the attitude. Try again... isn't it time you met someone?"

"Uh... sure. Absolutely."

"See?" She leaned her head on his shoulder. "That wasn't so hard, was it?"

He laughed, and kissed her on the forehead. "You're the best daughter in the world, you know that?"

She nodded sagely. "Remember that when you get my next report card, okay?"

"It's a deal."

"Right, that's enough emotional bonding for one day." She stood and headed for the door. "I'm going to make dinner, and you need to get changed. I know it's a lot to ask, but can you manage that yourself?"

"I can."

"Perfect. And remember, don't talk too much, okay? Ask lots of questions, and listen to her answers. And if all else fails... I dunno, talk about your stupid books or something."

"Gotcha," he said. "Talk about my awesome books."

"Oh, and don't cry in front of her. Women like sensitive men... but not on a first date."

"I wasn't planning on it," he said. "But I'll add it to my list."

"And one more thing, dad. Miss Wade's my favourite teacher." Her eyes narrowed. "So don't fuck it up."

~

Miss Wade arrived on time, which pleased Lucy.

A teacher should always lead by example.

She wore tight blue jeans and a satin blouse, and Lucy nodded in satisfaction at helping her dad choose the perfect outfit to complement her.

Miss Wade brought a bottle of wine, and insisted she couldn't drink because she had to drive home, which Lucy thought was sensible. The plan did not last long. By the time Lucy entered the living room to clear the table for dessert, the bottle was open and half-full, and Miss Wade's wineglass rim was stained with lipstick.

The conversation was flowing, though inevitably they were talking about her dad's books. Miss Wade fired questions at him about themes and ironic juxtapositions — whatever those were — while her dad struggled to remember character names in books he had written over two decades ago. When Lucy returned from the kitchen to serve bowls of mint choc-chip ice cream, Miss Wade was unloading paperbacks and hardbacks from a cardboard box and getting them individually signed.

Leaving the lovebirds to their ice cream and books, Lucy sat on her bed listening to music and eating a reheated bowl of leftover pasta. Between songs, easy laughter drifted up from downstairs.

It made her smile.

Tired from her duties as both chef *and* waiter, she considered going to bed early. But it had been ages since she had checked on Sammo, and if she hurried, she could be back before it got full dark.

Downstairs, Miss Wade was talking about the failed relationship that had led to her moving to the countryside, and it didn't feel appropriate to interrupt, so Lucy snuck out and wandered to the barn beneath rain clouds that glowered menacingly. Inside, she closed the barn door and put the lock in place. Not that she expected her dad to bring Miss W-ade out here, but... she guessed he would do *anything* to impress her.

Kinda like you inviting Rab round tomorrow?

Nope, that was totally different in about a million ways.

"Sammo?"

He wasn't there. She spotted the impression of his body on the hay by the generator, but Sammo himself was nowhere to be found.

"Where are you, buddy?"

She checked the various horse stalls. All empty. Up the ladder? Placing her hands on the rungs, she nervously started up. Rain pattered on the corrugated iron roof.

"Shit," she said, and jumped down. Sammo couldn't be up there anyway, she figured. The floor would have collapsed.

Thunder rumbled, and in the seconds it took her to reach the door, the rain turned into a torrential downpour that thrummed mightily against the roof and leaked through rusted holes.

Lucy looked down at her threadbare pyjama bottoms and baggy white Everclear tee. She couldn't get caught in that rain. Hell, she wasn't wearing a bra. What if Miss Wade saw her running home like a drowned rat? Or worse, her dad? She'd never live it down.

"Fucking Scotland," she grumbled, wishing they had moved to California instead. "I'll wait." A thunderstorm that heavy would burn itself out in a matter of minutes. In the meantime, she'd just have a wee lie down. She'd earned it.

Yawning, she kicked the hay into shape and snuggled in. The warmth of Sammo's body lingered, and she curled up.

"Only until it stops raining," she said, though she hadn't realised how tired she truly was. If she had, she would never have closed her eyes. For as the rain fell, and the sun dipped fully below the trees, something diabolical disturbed the darkness of the forest.

And this time, there was nothing to stop them.

19

———

IN HER DREAMS, LUCY HEARD IT.

Click-clack.

That awful sound.

Click-clack, click-clack.

She hated it.

Click-clack, click-clack, click-clack.

And when the remnants of the dream crumbled, and Lucy awoke from her fitful slumber, the first thing she did was open her eyes and wonder where the fuck she was. It was dark, and she couldn't find her covers, and her bed was strangely jagged.

No, not her bed.

Shit.

She was in the barn.

Light spits of rain drummed on the roof as she sat and brushed loose strands of hay from her hair. Keen to get back to her own soft mattress, she rose stiffly and lifted the plank from the doors, gently pushing one open.

Night had fallen. How long had she slept?

Sheltering in the doorway, she held one hand out to check the rain. It wasn't so bad. If she ran, she might—

Click-clack, click-clack.

Her stomach churned.

"No..."

Click-clack.

It was close.

The field was pitch black, the moon lost behind the clouds. All she had to orientate herself was a faint glow from between the living room curtains.

Click-clack, click-clack.

The farmhouse had never looked further away.

Frigid air nibbled at her skin. Could she make it? One of her dad's old jazz records played, which meant he was still up. Should she call for him? Or run?

Yes, run!

But with those monsters out there, running was a cosmic gamble she was unwilling to take. They *were* out there, weren't they? She gazed across the field, seeking movement and finding none. There were too many shadows, too many places to hide. Isn't that why the monsters came out at night? To blend with the darkness? Or were they afraid of light? She glanced from the generator up to the bare bulb dangling from the ceiling.

Stop wasting time and run for your life!

She was too scared.

The generator seemed her only hope, but she couldn't risk the noise.

Not now.

Not when she didn't know what was out there.

Run, you fool!

Where was Sammo? She needed his protection.

Dammit, if she'd run when she first opened the door,

she'd be home by now. Unless the monsters were lying in wait, ready to spring a trap?

Run run run run run!

She stepped out of the barn and felt the rain on her face.

So far, so good.

She took another step.

Click...

The area around the barn grew brighter, and she watched her shadow lengthen in the cool, pink glow.

Her shadow?

...clack.

All at once, the horror dawned on her. She had seen that lurid pink before, emanating from the inflating sac of—

She turned on her heels and leapt back inside, grabbing the door and slamming it shut as — *click-clack, click-clack* — the monster on the roof raced down the side of the barn. The door shook as sharp feet clattered against it. Lucy grabbed the plank of wood and slotted it into place as, through the gaps, the dark shape moved, sending splinters of pink light shooting through the interior.

She screamed, and then so did the creature, shrieking in a note perfect imitation of her own voice. Lucy stumbled backwards, tripping over her feet and landing hard. The monster battered the door, throwing its full weight against the entryway. A panel burst loose and fell to the floor, the pink glow seeping through the crack. She looked around for a weapon, for—

The pitchfork.

Yes!

She ran to where it hung and lifted the farming tool from its hook. It was taller than her, and top-heavy, so she held the wooden pole close to her body and shuffled towards the door.

The creature pounded against the wood.

"Sammo!" she shouted. "Dad!"

She needed help. Was she planning on fending off a monster with a pitchfork? Ridiculous. She was crying, and scared, and she'd never even been in a fight before.

She didn't stand a chance.

You did it before. In the woods, you helped Sammo. You killed one of them with your bare hands.

That was different. Back then, she had the element of surprise.

A glistening, skinless arm burst through the panels, the meaty red pincer on the end groping for the plank that held the doors shut.

"Fuck off!" Lucy shouted, and charged. She rammed the pitchfork through the gap, feeling the resistance as it stabbed into the monster's repulsive body. Hot, dark liquid fountained over her, dribbling down the wood as the creature screamed. Lucy dug her heels in and thrust the pitchfork deeper. The monster hurled itself from the barn, landing on the grass with a thump.

The room spun.

Click-clack, click-clack.

"Oh god."

She looked up.

The roof.

Click-clack, click-clack.

There were more of them *on the fucking roof.*

20

———————

In the near-darkness of the barn, Lucy Brannigan raised the pitchfork, black blood oozing down the steel prongs.

She had to defend herself.

How many were out there? Two? Ten? It was impossible to tell. In the pulse of the eerie pink glow, frantic shadows scurried across the roof and walls, seeking entry.

"Dad!" she yelled.

Why couldn't he hear her? Was his stupid fucking jazz music so loud?

More clicking above her. She whirled, trying to follow the sounds, but they were everywhere.

"Fuck off!" she shouted. Tossing the pitchfork onto the upper level, she climbed the ladder, the rotten wood crumbling in her hands. At the top, she grabbed the weapon. Footsteps rattled above her. She closed her eyes, concentrating on the sounds, and stabbed upwards. The prongs burst through the thin roof, but found nothing.

"Where are you, you fuck?"

Over there.

She moved stealthily, following the scratching of claws.

Gotcha.

She tried again, piercing the metal. The creature scuttled into the middle. Downstairs, limbs and putrid bodies hammered on the walls. More of them. Too many.

Recklessly, she thrust the pitchfork through the roof. This time, it stuck. The whatthefuck let out an unholy wail, and as Lucy yanked the weapon free, rivers of dark blood gushed through the newly created punctures in the corrugated iron.

"Got you!" she roared in triumph.

But so what? So fucking what? There were more outside, lurking in the darkness and trying to batter their way inside.

The darkness...

Surely — fucking *surely* — the generator would power the bulb? If so, it was her only chance. She dropped her weapon over the edge and scrambled down the ladder, as, all around her, the creatures broke through, throwing themselves against the wall and causing the barn to shake. What if they brought the whole thing down?

She cursed herself for falling asleep.

Wood cracked, and she turned to find ghoulish limbs scrabbling between the doors, a monster inching its body through one foul limb at a time. The pitchfork was too unwieldy, so she discarded it and wrenched the axe from the wall. With a feral scream, she brought the tarnished blade down on a groping, clawed limb. The axe head slammed into the meaty arm, the monster shrieking and retracting its spindly legs as Lucy yanked it free and hurried to the generator. She ran her hands over the contraption in search of an ON switch. Would it work? Would the light keep them at bay?

Maybe... and right now, maybe was enough.

She touched the metal, pressing at anything that felt like a button. Her fingertips brushed something soft and loose. A cord? She pulled on it, listening to the wheezing rasp of a motor.

"Yes!" she cried.

She tugged harder, and looked at the door. Whole panels had broken off, claws and reedy limbs scratching at the plank that secured the doors.

Sobbing, Lucy yanked the cord. The generator rumbled, almost catching... but didn't.

Maybe there's no fuel?

There would be. There *had* to be. The previous family had only moved out a couple of weeks ago, and she doubted they'd have left it empty.

Unless that's why they all died?

"Shut up."

To her right, the top half of the door exploded. Splinters of wood flew through the air and struck her. She didn't dare look.

"Come on!" she screamed, and pulled the cord so hard it burned her fingers.

The generator sputtered, then caught.

Above her, the lightbulb flickered into life.

It brightened...

...AND BRIGHTENED...

...AND BRIGHTENED...

. . .

...and then fizzled out with a muted pop, once more plunging the barn into gloom.

"Nooo!"

The generator chugged like a freight train, but it was all for naught. Her one light source — her only chance for survival — had failed.

A monster squeezed its body through the door and dropped to the ground. The fleshy pouch inflated, illuminating the barn and revealing the submerged freak inside, while beyond the four walls, the monsters' cacophonous wails tormented the night.

She considered giving up; closing her eyes and covering her ears and letting them come, letting them take her.

The thought only lasted a second. Sammo hadn't saved her life twice only for her to concede defeat.

Hunched over, and drenched in monster blood, she snatched up the axe and faced it. The fiend launched itself at her. She swung wildly, slamming the axe into the fat body, but the monster's velocity carried it onwards into a brutal collision. Lucy's head rocked back, and she hit the packed dirt.

The creature was on top of her.

She jerked the axe free, expelling another gout of blood. Claws scrabbled in the dirt and hay. The pink sac was out of reach, and in desperation, she leaned to the side and bit down on a thin limb. It felt like biting a stick, though the hard outer shell cracked under the pressure. The monster reared up. Lucy whacked the axe against its body, but she had little room to swing. One fleshy claw grasped for the blade and—

The monster screamed.

Three spikes burst through its body, coming to a sudden stop an inch from Lucy's face. Cold blood jetted from the ruptures, flooding over her, and then the monster was moving backwards against its will. Without thinking, Lucy scrambled to her feet, hacking at the exposed frame as, behind it, her dad twisted the pitchfork into the beast's back.

"*What the fuck, Lucy?*" he shouted.

"Hold it still!"

She swung the axe with both hands, over and over, lopping off limbs and avoiding the claws that gnashed fiercely before her eyes.

"Fuck you!" she yelled. "Fuck you!"

She chopped and hacked, bursting the monster open, its guts spilling onto the floor in moist coils. Her dad forced the beast to the ground and tugged the pitchfork free, letting it drop with a harsh clang.

Steam rose from the vile corpse. The limbs wilted, scraps of tissue flaking from the body as it disintegrated into a pool of acrid goop.

Lucy looked at her dad. Unblinking, he stared back at her.

"Are you okay?" he asked. "Are you hurt?"

"I'm fine," she said. "I think I—"

"*What the fuck is that?*"

Miss Wade stood in the doorway. She gripped the broken barn door for balance, and the shattered planks crumbled at her touch.

"That's... a monster," said Lucy, her pounding heart only now beginning to slow.

Miss Wade slid down the doorframe into a crouch. "But..."

"Monsters aren't real," said Lucy. Numbly, she wiped a sheen of blood from her face. "Yeah, that's what I used to think, until—"

"Quiet," her dad said. "You hear that?"

"What? I don't..."

Then she felt it. The ground shook as heavy footsteps thundered across the field. Her dad lifted the pitchfork. "Get inside," he barked at Miss Wade.

"What? What's happening?"

"Just get in!"

Lucy imagined it was a lot to take in for a person in their thirties. She picked up the axe and joined her father, as Miss Wade stumbled into the barn in a state of shock.

The footsteps drew nearer.

Thu-doom, thu-doom.

Closer and closer.

The pitchfork trembled in her dad's hands.

Any moment now...

"Wait," said Lucy. A smile broke out across her face, and she lowered the axe. She recognised the sound of those clumsy paws.

"Sammo!" she shouted, and as the lumbering oaf entered through the shattered remains of the door, Lucy threw her arms around his chunky body. His fur was coated in fresh, dark blood.

"It's another one!" shrieked Miss Wade.

"It's okay," her dad explained. "It's Sammo."

"That's not a fucking horse, Brian!"

Lucy ignored them and snuggled into Sammo, losing herself in her friend's warm embrace.

"Lucy?" her dad called, his voice distant, dreamlike.

She wanted to reply, but couldn't.

The adrenaline was wearing off.

Her eyes closed, and her body went limp in Sammo's paws.

She was so very, very tired.

21

———

Lucy had never believed in God.

Her parents had rarely set foot in church, and brought her up to question beliefs, encouraging her to make up her own mind regarding spiritual matters. She had thought about it, decided that the idea of an all-powerful being was a bit far-fetched, and never considered it again.

But she hadn't believed in monsters either, so when she opened her eyes in the living room and found herself face-to-face with an angel — a beautiful, heavenly angel — she simply accepted it.

The angel, her golden hair shimmering, placed a celestial hand on Lucy's forehead.

"Where are your wings?" croaked Lucy.

"Pardon?"

She tried to blink away her blurred vision. "An angel should have wings. So they can fly."

The angel smiled at her, and stroked her hair. "Sorry. I'm just an art teacher."

"Huh?"

"Brian," shouted the angel. *"She's coming around!"*

Lucy tried to sit, her head swooning. "Miss Wade?"

"It's me, Lucy." She handed her a glass of water. "Here, sip this."

The cool liquid hurt her throat, and she realised she had she just called her teacher an angel. Oh, for fuck's sake. And she had been worried about her *dad* embarrassing her.

He entered the room, grappling with a jacket, his arm in the wrong sleeve. "How is she?"

"She's okay. Woozy, I'd say. She called me an angel."

"Right." He was barely listening. "Shall we take my van?"

"No, I'll drive. I know where I'm going, and I've had less to drink." She sighed. "To be honest, I've never felt more sober."

Going? Where were they going? Lucy looked up at her dad. "What's happening? How's Sammo?"

"Lucy, we're taking you to see a doctor. You need—"

"You're not taking me anywhere! I need to check on Sammo." She attempted to stand, but it was too soon. Waves of nausea washed over her, and she planted her feet on the carpet and waited for them to pass.

"You're in shock," her dad said.

"I'm fine. But they might have hurt Sammo. I'm not leaving him behind."

"Lucy, you need medical attention. We can bring a doctor back to check on him. Or a vet, I don't know."

"You really should see a doctor," said Miss Wade.

"Don't give me that!" They were ganging up on her. "I'm not hurt. I defended myself."

Her dad's face was pale, and splattered with blood. He discarded the jacket and knelt by her. "I know you did," he said, and took her hand. "But Lucy... what *was* that thing?"

～

For Miss Wade's benefit, she started from the beginning. From her first encounter with Sammo in his nest, to finding the tunnels, right up until the barn attack. They listened in disbelief, and only interrupted once or twice.

"Sammo keeps them away," she said, as she neared the end of her tale. "Rab told me about a Guardian of the Forest, who protects Helsbridge from the monsters. I think he was talking about Sammo." She looked her dad straight in the eyes. "Put *that* in your story."

"Maybe I will," he said, and turned to Miss Wade. "Any of this make sense to you?"

"Why would it?"

"You've lived here longer than us."

"Six *months* longer." She relaxed into her chair and sipped her wine. "But yeah, from the stories I've heard, it tracks with what people round here believe. It's not some dark secret. Shit, it's all anyone from Helsbridge talks about. I just never thought for a second that... that any of it was true."

"We have to go to the police," her dad said. "Is there a station in Helsbridge?"

"No police," snapped Lucy. "You promised you wouldn't tell anyone."

"For Christ's sake, this is serious! We've got a monster in our barn, and you just got attacked by... by..."

She touched his arm. "Dad, there's no point telling anyone. Miss Wade said everyone around here *knows* monsters are real, right? But they don't know what they *look* like. If you show them Sammo, they'll think he's to blame. They'll kill him."

"You don't know—"

"I *do* know, dad. You read Frankenstein to me when I was little, remember?"

"*Really*, Brian?" asked Miss Wade.

They both ignored her. It had been a great bedtime story.

"Then we'll tell them the truth," her dad said. "We'll explain that—"

"You think they'll believe us?"

"She's got a point," Miss Wade interjected. "We're all newcomers, and the only thing Helsbridgers hate more than monsters is outsiders. They're a very, uh, *insular* community."

Her dad shook his head incredulously. "You're taking her side?"

"It's not about sides," said Miss Wade. "It's about doing the right thing. And maybe Lucy's correct in thinking they'd kill... I'm sorry, what was his name again?"

"Sammo," said Lucy, her admiration for Miss Wade only growing.

"That's right, Sammo. And if she's also right about Sammo keeping the monsters at bay, then what would happen if they *do* kill him? The whole town — including us — would be fucked." Miss Wade blushed. "Pardon my language."

"I can't believe I'm hearing this," Lucy's dad said. "I'd expect this from a teenager, but not you. Not her *teacher*."

"Well I'm sorry to disappoint you, Brian, but your daughter's right. If Sammo really is the..." — she struggled to get the words out, as if she had trouble believing them — "...the *Guardian of the Forest*, then we have to take care of him."

Her dad emptied his wine glass. "And what about Lucy? She needs a doctor. Look at her!"

Lucy glanced down at her blood-drenched clothes. "Oh,

none of that's mine," she said. "That belongs to those whatthefucks I killed."

Her dad looked at her, then down at his empty glass. "I need another fucking drink," he said, and left the room.

Lucy went for a shower, and to stop her dad bleating on about seeing a doctor, she invited Miss wade to accompany her to the bathroom. There, she disrobed and let her teacher check she was physically unharmed from her fight. It wasn't as embarrassing as she thought — she kept her knickers on, at least — and once it was over, Miss Wade took her bloody clothes and left her alone, on the understanding that Lucy did not lock the door.

Beneath the warm jets of water, she watched the blood and scum swirl down the plughole. She hoped her dad understood she wasn't *trying* to be difficult, but there was no way she could abandon Sammo. She owed him, big time. Everyone in town did, even if they didn't realise it.

Feeling refreshed, she put on her bathrobe and rejoined her dad and Miss Wade in the living room.

"Okay," he was saying, seemingly under the impression he was in charge. "So the consensus seems to be that we tell no one, and look after Sammo ourselves. Is that correct?"

"Yup," said Lucy.

"Uh-huh. Meanwhile, we live in the same field where my daughter was attacked by rampaging spider-crabs—"

"Whatthefucks," Lucy interrupted.

"Okay, in the same field where my daughter was attacked by rampaging whatthefucks. That's our plan?"

"You have a better one?" asked Miss Wade.

"Yeah, actually, I do. We get the fuck out of here. We get in the van and drive, and we don't stop until—"

"Drive where?" asked Lucy. "We're broke, remember?"

"The money doesn't matter," he said, his voice cracking. "All I care about is keeping you safe." He wiped a sleeve across his eyes, tears streaking his cheeks. Miss Wade placed her hand on his knee.

"Dad," Lucy whispered. He looked at her through splayed fingers. "I told you not to cry on a first date."

He was silent for a moment... and then he laughed. Miss Wade joined in, and kissed his head as he laughed and cried into her shoulder.

Lucy smiled to herself.

Maybe crying *was* okay on a first date. But, she supposed, only if earlier in the evening you had killed a monster with a pitchfork to save your daughter. Then — and *only* then, she decided, as her own eyes filled with tears, and she joined them on the couch — was crying on a first date acceptable.

With Miss Wade washing up in the bathroom, Lucy and her dad sat alone for the first time that evening. A jazz record spun on the turntable. *April in Paris* by Charlie Parker, according to the LP jacket. It all sounded the same to her.

"You should get some sleep," he said, stifling a yawn. "We all should."

"Yeah," said Lucy. Her body told her she was exhausted, yet her brain was wide awake. From outside, she heard the distant *putt-putt* of the generator. "I'll go in a minute."

Nothing felt real. Sitting with her dad, the music play-ing... it could be any nondescript day of the week. She had nearly died tonight, and here they were, getting ready for bed as if nothing had happened. If her dad hadn't appeared in time, would the monster have killed her? Or could she have held it off until Sammo arrived? Come to think of it, where had Sammo been? She assumed he'd sensed the monsters' presence and raced off into the forest. Perhaps they'd lured him away from the barn? She hoped they weren't that clever. The only thing she was certain of was that Sammo had chased off the rest of the monsters. She had definitely heard more than one climbing the walls.

But wait... hadn't her dad reached the barn several minutes *before* Sammo?

Fuck, nothing made sense.

"Dad, did you see any other monsters on your way to the barn?"

"Nope. Just the one."

"And you're sure Sammo's okay?"

"He's fine, Lucy."

She eyed him suspiciously. "For real?"

"He had some nicks and cuts when he came in. They didn't look deep, though."

"I'm going to see him first thing tomorrow."

"As soon as the sun's up," he said. She didn't argue. Hell, she was never venturing out in the dark again.

Her dad refilled his wine glass. "Need something to help you sleep?"

Too tired to reply, she nodded, and he half-filled Miss Wade's glass and handed it to her.

"I want you to know," he said, "that I'm proud of you."

"What for?"

"For everything. If it was up to me, we'd be five hundred miles away by now. I never even considered the people who live around here. I guess because you're my daughter, and you're all I have left. But you... you understood that Sammo protects Helsbridge. The fact you'd put your own life at risk for people you've never even met is pretty, well... astounding."

Honestly, she'd been more concerned with Sammo's wellbeing than the townsfolk, but she accepted the compliment. "That's just the kinda gal I am."

"And then arriving at the barn and seeing you fighting off that monster with an axe..." He half-smiled. "Guess you're not a kid anymore, huh?"

"Haven't been for a long time," she said. "And hey, you weren't so bad yourself. You didn't even hesitate. Okay, so you almost stabbed me in the face with a pitchfork, but... I've never seen you like that before."

"I saved your life," he said.

"Let's not go that far. I had everything under control."

"Like hell you did. You owe me one."

"Calm down, dad," she said, finishing her wine. "You only did it to impress Miss Wade."

"You think it worked?"

She laughed, and got up from the settee. "I'm going to bed. Give my teacher a goodnight snog for me, would ya?"

"Don't be cheeky."

She kissed his stubbled cheek. "Night, dad."

"Wait," he said. "One more question, if you don't mind."

She wasn't in the mood — her bed was calling to her — but she supposed she *did* owe him one.

"Shoot."

"How did you know it would work?" he asked.

"How *what* would work?"

"The generator."

"But it didn't. The bulb blew."

"The bulb?" He looked as confused as she was. "I'm not talking about the bulb. I'm talking about the scarecrows."

"Dad, I'm too tired for this."

"You... you really don't know, do you?" He walked towards the window and drew back the curtain. "I'm talking about *this.*"

In a daze, Lucy joined him at the window.

"What the fuck...?"

Unable to believe her eyes, she stared out in awe. Was she seeing things? This couldn't be real.

The scarecrows... they were *alive.*

The mannequin on the bicycle peddled furiously, his legs pumping. A child spun on the spot, pirouetting in the sickly moonlight. Two cowboys raised and lowered six-shooters from their hips, while the butcher's fist shook with mechanical precision. Even the pug's curly tail wagged back and forth.

"Oh my god," she said, as the sudden evacuation of the whatthefucks began to make sense.

"Pretty neat, eh?" her dad said. "Must've been the family who lived here's last line of defence."

"Must've been," she agreed, as the demented display continued on an endless loop. "How long will it last?"

"There's plenty fuel."

She glanced at the barn. One of the doors blew in the wind, the other lying in pieces on the ground.

"Good," she said, the chug of the generator competing with the lazy rhythms of her dad's music. "Keep it going, day and night." She rested her forehead against the glass and imagined the mannequins were dancing. "Don't ever switch it off."

22

———————

THE FIRST THING LUCY DID THE NEXT MORNING WAS CHECK out her window.

The field was alive with activity as the scarecrows moved and spun and swayed in a surreal ballet. She opened the window and leaned out. The dewy grass glistened, and the air smelt of pine.

Summer was officially here, and last night felt a million years away.

She put on some cycling shorts and a poorly printed bootleg *Gish* tee-shirt, and crept through the hallway, drawn by the repetitive sounds of her dad's typing and the frequent *ding* of the typewriter bell. When she peeked around the door, he didn't notice her.

"Morning, dad."

"Huh?"

"I said morning. You had breakfast?"

He glanced up at the suggestion of food. "No, not yet."

"Working on that new story?"

His fingers never slowed. "You bet! The words are just

pouring out." He pulled the sheet from the machine and laid it on a pile beneath a paperweight lighthouse.

"Cool," she said. "I'm fine, by the way."

"What?"

"After I nearly died last night. I'm fine, thanks for asking."

"Of course. You sure?"

"Yup. What's happening in your story?"

He paused to pick up a pencil and chew thoughtfully on the eraser. "Umm, the daughter was attacked in the barn by monsters."

"Uh-huh. Where *do* you get your ideas?"

He chuckled and resumed typing.

"So," said Lucy. "Did the daughter manage to defend herself?"

"No," he said without looking at her. "She peed her pants."

"She *what?*"

"Don't worry." He grinned. "Her dad came to the rescue and killed three of them with a shotgun."

"That doesn't sound very believable."

"Believability is the coward's way out. Whereas I," he said, his fingers dextrously blurring across the keys, "am an artist unconstrained by bourgeois notions of rationality."

"You're such a loser. So what's the ending?"

"The ending? I'm not quite there. It's gonna have to be a good one. Give me time, and I'll—"

But she had stopped listening. "Hey, did I leave my hairspray in your room last night?"

"What? I don't know, go check. I'm busy."

She shrugged and wandered the length of the hallway. His bedroom door was closed, and as she gripped the handle, she heard him shout.

"Wait, Lucy, don't go in there!"

Too late. The door was already swinging open.

"Oh shit," she said, for it was not every day she found her high school art teacher lying face down on her dad's bed in nothing but a pair of lacy red knickers. Miss Wade turned at the sound of her voice. She stared at Lucy, unsure what to do, and Lucy stared back, too stunned to move.

"My... hairspray," she managed to say, and pointed at the canister.

The words galvanised Miss Wade into action.

"Oh god, I'm so sorry!" the woman cried, and scrambled off the bed with her arm across her chest. She ran for the en-suite bathroom and slammed the door, shouting, *"I'm sorry, I'm sorry!"*

Lucy grabbed her hairspray, and said, "Uh, I'm also sorry." As she beat a hasty retreat to her room, she passed her dad in the hallway.

"Lucy, wait," he said. "You weren't meant to—"

"Can't talk," she spluttered, her embarrassed giggles threatening to erupt into full-blown hilarity. She made it to her room and collapsed onto the bed in gales of laughter.

A few minutes later came the unavoidable knock at the door.

"Lucy? May we come in?"

She took a breath, composed herself, and said, in her poshest voice, "You may."

The door opened, and her dad sheepishly entered, Miss Wade lurking behind him. Her teacher had dressed in a hurry — the buttons on her blouse were done up incorrectly — but she spoke first.

"Lucy, I want to apologise for... for what you saw. We never intended to..."

"What Elli is trying to say," her dad interrupted, "is that

we were all a little shaken up by last night, and we'd been drinking... what I mean is, we couldn't *drive* because we'd been drinking, not that we... *did* anything... because we were drunk..."

"Okay," said Lucy, stifling more giggles.

"What happened last night," said Miss Wade, "was that... two adults, who enjoy each other's company, and who had both experienced a shock..."

"Mm-hmm," said Lucy. "You want to finish that sentence?"

"No one is trying to replace your mother," blurted her dad, and Miss Wade looked aghast.

"Guys," said Lucy, "Just stop. Both of you. I want to eat my breakfast, so let's get this straight. Miss Wade, my dad *clearly* fancies you. That's why *I* invited you round for dinner, not him, because if you were waiting for him, you'd be two-hundred years old by the time he asked. And, Miss Wade... I know you fancy my dad, because I saw your knickers, and from one woman to another, you only wear underwear like that on a date when you *want* somebody to see them." She gazed at their blank faces. "Now, are we done here?"

"Yeah," her dad said, a sly smile spreading across his face.

"Good." She sauntered between them and stopped at the top of the stairs. "Assuming I can leave you two unattended, yeah?"

"Go make breakfast," her dad said, though he was trying not to laugh. "Or you're grounded for a month."

"Okay, dad." She jogged down the stairs, and, as a parting gift, shouted, *"Hope you used protection!"*

～

Miss Wade surreptitiously left while Lucy was waiting on her toast.

She considered going upstairs to further embarrass her dad, but he was typing, and she decided to let him work. Maybe this monster story could be the bestseller he'd been chasing?

She wouldn't hold her breath.

Instead, she went to the barn, hoping to find Sammo. She rushed past the mechanical scarecrows and stepped over the broken door. Inside, the pitchfork and the axe lay beside a pool of black goo that had once been a monster. Nothing corporeal remained other than a few fragile bones submerged in the thick paste.

"Sammo? Are you there?"

The wind whistled through the broken wood.

"Sammo?"

Had he returned to his nest? If so, and he was back to full strength, then it really was foolish of them to stay in the farmhouse. Smart people would leave immediately.

And do what? There was nowhere to go. They couldn't afford a flat, or even a hotel, and they certainly couldn't live in the van, driving from town to town and crying themselves to sleep next to their broken TV. No money meant no options.

No way out.

She was depressing herself, so she left the miserable confines of the barn and stared at the forest. Would she ever see Sammo again? Perhaps not, and though her heart would break, she would understand. He was a warrior — the *Guardian of the Forest* — and he had better things to do than waste time being petted. Granted, he was a very cuddly warrior, with a squishy-wishy face and soft, luxurious fur... but a warrior he remained.

When she slunk back into the house, her dad was in the kitchen making coffee. "Want some?" he asked.

"Sammo's gone," she replied glumly.

"I'm sure he'll be back. He's probably off pooping. You notice he never went in the barn?" He poured hot water into his mug. "Thank god, that's all I can say."

She leaned against the counter. "Dad, do you think we should leave?"

"Leave? Last night you *insisted* we stay!"

"I know. But I'm asking for your opinion. That doesn't happen often, so take advantage."

"Hmmm. Well, if you're asking, then I say… we stay. Just for a little while, until I finish my new book. I'm inspired, Luce. A new start, a new home, surrounded by monsters… I don't remember the last time I felt this alive. Now, if I thought we were in danger, I'd get us out of here, pronto. But with Sammo around, and—"

"The scarecrows," Lucy finished. "Yeah, cool. For once, we agree."

"Good." He sipped his coffee. It was hot, and he winced as it scalded his lip. "Anyway, it would be a shame to leave now, just as I'm getting to know Elli."

"And there it is," said Lucy. "The *real* reason." She patted her dad on the arm and wandered upstairs to decide what the hell was she going to do all day. She gazed out the window at the mountains. With no Sammo, and the woods out-of-bounds, she was trapped here.

Click-clack.

Her spine tingled.

Click-clack, click-clack, click-clack.

It wasn't possible.

The sun was out, and it was a beautiful day, and the scarecrows—

"Lucy!"

She looked down, and there was Rab cycling in circles below her window, the playing cards tucked into the spokes of his bicycle making an insistent *click-clack* noise.

"You motherfucker," she whispered, her heart pounding in her chest. Then she started to laugh, and waved back. "I'll be right down!"

23

"Pretty convenient, eh?" laughed Rab. "I come round tae see your monster, and he's fucked off intae the woods."

"He *was* here," Lucy said. "He left this morning."

They stood in the empty barn, staring at some abandoned farming tools and a puddle of black goo that Rab insisted was, as he so delicately put it, *liquid shite*.

"I swear it," she said. "We can ask my dad."

"Nah, yer awright. So, whaddya wannae do?"

She wasn't sure. After the events of last night, she'd forgotten Rab was even coming round, and with Sammo gone, there was nothing *to* do.

"We could go for a walk?"

"Through the woods, aye? Sure, if ya want tae *die.*"

"You got a better idea?"

"We could go up tae your room and listen tae some tunes?"

"No," she said quickly. For a start, she hadn't tidied since the day they'd moved in, and her clothes were strewn across the floor and furniture. Secondly, it felt too intimate to sit on her bed with a boy she hardly knew, albeit one she was developing a weird crush on.

Rab, to his credit, seemed unfazed by the dismissal. He turned his face towards the sun. "It's a nice day. You been tae Helsbridge Loch?"

"Where's that?"

"Helsbridge," he said. She supposed the clue *was* in the name. "It's past the town. The locals go there tae swim, if ya fancy that? Might even be able tae chore some cunt's booze."

"Sounds good," she said. "How do we get there?"

Rab pointed at his bike and grinned. "I can give you a lift!"

He waited outside while she ran upstairs to change into her swimsuit, which she wore beneath a blue gingham summer dress. She told her dad where she was going, promised to return long before dark, and hopped on the back of Rab's BMX.

"Hold on tight," he said, and pedalled off, dodging potholes and showing-off by speeding up along the main road. Lucy had to wrap her arms around him to feel safe, but she assumed he didn't mind. The wind blew her hair, and she felt like a child again. When was the last time she had ridden a bicycle?

Helsbridge passed in the blink of an eye, and after another mile or so, Rab took a sharp right through a field, passing cottages and trees until they came to a large body of water. Several young people were there already, laughing and shouting and splashing about, while different stereos competed for attention, one playing *Return of the Mack,* another blaring Babylon Zoo's

Spaceman. Rab cycled past them all, finding a secluded spot near the trees.

There, they dismounted the bike and sat together on the stony beach, slagging off everyone else's poor taste in music. Rab asked if she wanted to swim, but Lucy, too shy to be seen in her swimsuit, refused. They lay in the sun, sharing a can of Pepsi and talking for hours.

Inevitably, after in-depth discussions on the best Smashing Pumpkins songs and who would be better live, Hole or L7, the conversation turned to monsters.

"You really tellin' me you had one livin' in your barn?"

"Honestly," said Lucy. Sweat dripped down her shoulders. God, she wanted nothing more than to take a dip in the cool water.

"Yer no shiteing me?"

"He was there. My dad saw him too. *And* Miss Wade."

"Whit, the art teacher? Why was she roond?"

Lucy realised she'd said too much. She didn't want to get Miss Wade in trouble. "Uh, she came round to tell my dad I'd skipped school."

"That's shan."

"Yeah, I guess. But she saw Sammo, and she was cool with him."

"Aye, she's mostly sound, like. No bad lookin, either."

"Rab!" snapped Lucy.

He turned to her, grinning. "Jealous, are ya?"

She rolled onto her front to avoid his gaze. "No. I just... she's so old. She's like, *forty* or something."

"As long as yer no jealous."

"I'm *not* jealous."

"Good."

"Fine." She stole a glance at him, and when their eyes met, butterflies danced in her stomach.

Rab looked away. "It's fuckin' boiling," he said. "I'm going in." He pulled his tee-shirt off, revealing his pale, skinny body, then unbuckled his belt. Lucy watched him remove his tracky bottoms, pulling them down over surprisingly brawny legs.

Must be from all that cycling, she thought.

"Well?" he asked. "You comin' in, or ya just gonnae stare at ma legs?"

Her cheeks burned. "I wasn't staring."

"Aye right," he laughed, and paddled into the loch in his lurid neon swim shorts. "Aw, it's fuckin' freezing!" he laughed, and waded further until he tripped and fell below the surface. He rose, water pouring off him, and shouted, "Come on in!"

Fuck it.

"Fine!" she said, and with her heart racing, she unbuttoned her dress and lifted it over her head. Her blue swimsuit wasn't revealing, but it was as undressed as she'd ever been in front of a boy she fancied.

Fancied?

Yeah, why not? He was a dufus, but also nice and funny and with great taste in music. Plus, he had muscular legs and a kind, genuine smile. She tugged her swimsuit as far as it would go to cover her bum, and—

"Hey, new girl."

Oh, for fuck's sake. Not Isobel, not today!

She turned to face the bully, who looked immaculate in a black string bikini and sunglasses, an ice cold bottle of *Becks* in her hand. Her dark hair hung flawlessly over tanned shoulders.

Tanned? How the hell did a Scottish girl get a tan?

Lucy looked for Rab, but he was splashing in the water

like an idiot. Instinctively, she crossed her arms over her chest. "What do you want?"

"I'm not here to be a bitch," said Isobel. She offered her the beer. "I brought you this, that's all."

Baffled, Lucy stared at the bottle.

"Go on, take it. It's a peace offering."

It had to be a trap.

Lucy cautiously reached out and took the beer. It was delightfully chilly, and the condensation trickled through her fingers.

"Thanks," she said. Was the bottle full of piss?

Isobel half-shrugged. "I just wanted to say, I'm sorry about the other day. In the forest, y'know. We shouldn't have left you behind. We got scared, that's all. The monsters don't usually come out that far."

Lucy stared dumbly at her.

"How did you get away?" asked Isobel.

Careful now. Don't involve Sammo. Make something up.

"I... I don't know. I fell out of the tree, and when I woke up, I went home."

Jeez, something more exciting than that!

"You're lucky," said Isobel. "But I guess it's cool you didn't die."

"Uh, thank you."

Isobel glanced at her brother. "By the way, Rab won't shut up about you, so don't mess him around. He's a dick, but he's still my brother."

"I won't."

"So, we're cool, aye?"

"Yeah. Super-duper cool," she replied, cringing at her words.

"You're a real nerd," said Isobel with the hint of a smile. "I get what my brother sees in you."

With that, she left.

Unsure what the hell had just happened, Lucy laid the bottle in the sand — she hated beer — and watched Isobel return to her friends. She noticed the girl walked with a limp, favouring her left leg.

Rab waded to the beach and stood shivering beside her. "Here, what did *she* want?"

"Nothing, really," said Lucy, still puzzled by the interaction. "She brought me a beer."

"Fuckin' barry!" He picked up the bottle and took a long drink. "So she's no causing trouble?"

"Nope. She was quite... nice, actually."

"She used tae always be like that. Then she had the accident, and after that she changed." He held the bottle to his lips and downed the remainder.

"Changed? In what way?"

He tossed the bottle on the sand. "She became a right cunt."

Lucy chuckled. "Well, everything's cool between us now."

Super-duper cool, apparently.

She turned to Rab, feeling better about herself than she had in years. "Come on," she said, and playfully shoved him. "Race you into the loch!"

Hours later, they cycled home, still wearing their swimming costumes. In her excitement, Lucy had forgotten to bring a towel or underwear to change into, and she sure as shit wasn't going to go commando on a bicycle. She clung to Rab, letting the warm, rushing air dry her skin. Spending time with him was fun. He made her laugh. A lot. She had found boys physically attractive before — and some girls — but she had never met one who could make her knees go funny just by *talking* to her.

She leaned her head against him and smiled. If it wasn't for all the monsters, this had the potential to be the best summer of her life. Maybe it still could? With Sammo back in action, and the curfew in place, the monsters might just... give up? Move elsewhere?

Unlikely, but it wouldn't stop her from dreaming.

They arrived at her house with enough time for Rab to get home before the curfew. He rested the bike against the farmhouse wall and looked at her awkwardly, as if trying to think of something to say.

"I had a nice day," she told him.

"Aye? Me too."

"Even your sister was okay."

"Aye," grinned Rab. "That's cos she's babysitting tonight, and she and her boyfriend are gonnae..." He made a circle with the fingers of one hand and jabbed his index finger repeatedly through the middle. "She'll be pure cheesin' about it."

Lucy pulled a face, and he stopped.

"Sorry," he said. "Sometimes I cannae help myself."

"It's alright. Never change."

"What, you dinnae want me to be all normal and boring?"

"Normal is overrated," she said.

"Aye, it is." He took a lumbering step closer. Was he going to do it? Lucy closed her eyes. He'd fucking better, or else she'd look like a right plum, standing there with—

Yes!

Rab kissed her. Her legs wobbled, and she put her hands on his waist to steady herself. It wasn't her first kiss — okay, it was her second — but it was definitely the best. Tentative hands reached for her lower back and lingered there. Their tongues brushed together, and only when Rab's fingers slid down to her bum did she stop him. She might have let him cop a feel if she was wearing more than a swimsuit.

"Uh-uh," she said, breaking the kiss. "That'll do now for now," she added with a smile.

"Aye, awright," he said, blushing. She saw movement below his waist, and he quickly turned away, muttering, "Sorry."

She giggled. "It's okay. Does this mean you like me?"

"Uh, aye," he said, still standing with his back to her. "I'd better get home. Before curfew, like."

He sidestepped towards his bike and got on. "Wannae hang out tomorrow?" he asked without looking at her.

"I'd love to," she said.

"Cool." He got on his bike.

"Bye, Rab." She ran to him, gave him a quick peck on the cheek, then peeked at the bulge in his shorts.

"Oi!" he squeaked, covering himself with his hands, and she ran into the house and closed the front door, leaning against the solid wood. There, she sucked in big lungfuls of air, then raced to the kitchen and opened the window as Rab cycled past.

Click-clack, click-clack.

"I saw it!" she called out the open window.

"Saw what?" asked her dad, and Lucy screamed.

"Don't sneak up on me like that!" she shouted, and ran, laughing and exhilarated, to her room.

That night, after dinner, she visited the barn. It was getting dark, so her dad accompanied her. Sammo wasn't there, which upset her, but at least the generator still had over half a tank of gas.

As they walked back to the house beneath a blood-red sky, her dad told her Miss Wade was coming round again tomorrow night, and asked if Lucy could make dinner.

"Sure," she said distractedly, and glanced at the unquiet darkness of the forest. "Dad... you ever wish things could stay the way they are forever?"

She thought he might dismiss her question, but he seemed to give it serious consideration.

"I used to," he replied. "Then, for a while, I wished things could go back to how they were. Now, I just hope it'll get better."

"I hear you," she said. "But I think you have to keep going, because sometimes you find happiness in the most unexpected places, don't you?"

"What's made you so philosophical?"

"Dunno." She hooked her arm around his waist. "I love you, dad."

"I love you too, Luce," he said, and they walked the rest of the way in silence, a father and a daughter, both feeling like they finally belonged somewhere, and both blissfully, *painfully* unaware of the nightmare that awaited them.

In twenty-four hours, it would all be over.

24

Isobel Macleod stepped out of the shower and wrapped a towel around herself. She disliked showering in someone else's home, but tonight she had no choice. From the clouded mirror, her flushed, wet face stared back at her.

She was officially a woman now.

"Was that it?" she asked her reflection.

Isobel had offered her virginity to PC James O'Neill, and he had taken it gratefully. Or, more accurately, *greedily*. Did it always hurt like that? If so, she was glad the ordeal lasted less than a minute.

Afterwards, she had lain on the bed in discomfort and watched him throw on his clothes. "Better go to work," he had mumbled, and then he was out the door and gone before he even had his fly zipped. Had it been as unsatisfying for him? She worried she was to blame. But it was *her* first time, not his. She needed guidance, and the gentle caress of a loving hand... not the nicotine stink of his breath as he grunted in her face.

And what about foreplay? Wasn't that something lovers engaged in? Once her clothes were off, he had forced his way inside her without a word. It hurt, and she had bled a little, and now she stood, cold and naked and staring at her reflection.

Better go to work.

Where was the romance?

In her mind, after the expected fireworks, they would have snuggled while James whispered sweet nothings into her ears. But no. He had to rush off to Auchenmullan to threaten drunks and ogle teenagers in short skirts on their way to The Vault nightclub.

It wasn't fair. Conditions had been perfect. She had put little Florence to bed at eight, and switched on the porch light to signal James, who was waiting around the corner in his police cruiser. He parked around the side of the building in case anyone passed by, and then they shared a tipple, but the anticipation had been too great, and they quickly headed upstairs to the spare room. Minutes later, he was gone, and she was alone with a slumbering toddler.

She checked in on Florence — the little girl was sleeping soundly — and padded across the hallway to the spare room. Numbly, she dried and dressed herself in loose, comfortable clothing. Something wet squelched beneath her foot, and she looked in horror at the used condom on the carpet.

"Fuck you, James," she hissed. She had planned to spend this evening in the throes of passionate ecstasy, not smearing semen off the soles of her newly washed feet. Feeling sorry for herself, Isobel tucked the slimy rubber in the bin beneath some rubbish and trudged downstairs. There was nothing good on the telly, so she watched the second half of *A Touch of Frost* without paying attention, wondering what James was up to. Was he thinking about her? About how to make it up to her, and show her what sex *really* was? She doubted it.

Wham, bam, thank you, ma'am.

Conscious of the time, Isobel walked back upstairs to check they hadn't left any more incriminating evidence in the spare room.

The first thing that hit her was the pungent odour of stale sex.

She opened the window to air the room, and gazed out across the fields. It was raining heavily, and she was glad to have gotten a glimpse of summer that afternoon at the loch.

Below her, the rain drummed against something metallic. She peered down at the source of the noise.

James's police car was still there.

"What the *fuck.*"

He had left, what, ninety minutes ago? Why was his fucking car still parked outside? If the Richardsons saw that when they came home, they'd freak out.

She hurried down the stairs. The stupid bastard had probably fallen asleep in his cruiser. So not only was he going to get *her* in trouble, he'd be in deep shit with the chief. She opened the front door and hesitated as the torrential rain battered the porch. Her light sweater would offer no protection, so she grabbed Mr Richardson's green waterproof off the peg and slung it over her head.

Raindrops thrummed off the jacket as she scurried around the building, her feet sliding on the slick pathway.

"I'll fucking kill him," she muttered, as she rounded the corner and strode towards the car. Heavy rainfall turned the windows into plunging waterfalls, obscuring the interior, and she pounded on the driver's side. "Hey, prickface! Wake up!"

No answer. She grabbed the handle and yanked the door open.

There was nobody inside.

"James?"

Where the hell was he? The Richardsons could be home any minute now! Shielding her eyes from the rain, she saw something lying on the path further down the lane.

A smart black shoe belonging to James.

She closed the car door and headed closer, stooping to pick the footwear up. The shoe was heavier than expected, and when she turned it over, and saw the meaty flesh of his ankle, and the cleanly snapped bone nestled amongst the blood and gristle, she couldn't even scream.

Terror had taken her voice.

She backed away, the shoe falling from her hand.

It's a joke, it's a joke, she told herself. *He's playing a mean trick.*

She bumped into the car and let out an almighty scream.

From nearby, someone answered with an appalling shriek of their own. It was a sound she knew, for she had heard it before, coming from within the woods.

And with that revelation, there was no doubt in her mind.

The monsters were here.

They had killed James, and now they would come for her. Wasting no more time, she ran around the car and headed for the front door. She thought she saw movement in her periphery, but the rain made it hard to tell, and as she reached the door... she realised she had left it wide open.

"Oh god," she muttered.

They could be inside already.

She shrugged off the raincoat and bounded up the stairs to Florence's room. The bedroom door was closed.

A promising sign.

Fighting the urge to barge through, she swept silently in and gazed down at the toddler. Still there, and still fast asleep.

Thank god.

Now, she needed to call the police.

Shit.

The phone was in the hallway at the bottom of the stairs.

Isobel swallowed hard. Could she barricade herself and Florence in the bedroom and wait it out until the Richardsons came home? That seemed the most sensible option. With the child snoozing peacefully, Isobel pressed her ear to the door.

Click-clack, click-clack.

Her heart sank.

They were here. They were inside.

It's fine. We can wait.

Her legs trembled. Her whole body did.

The *My Little Pony* clock on the wall said it was ten-to-eleven. Ten minutes until Florence's folks were due home. She could hang on.

She had to.

Click-clack, click-clack.

The noise came from down the stairs. She opened the door a crack, and when the phone unexpectedly rang, she had to bite down on her fist to stop from screaming. She looked at Florence, internally pleading with the little girl not to wake. The phone rang once, twice, three times... and then the answering machine tape took over.

"Hi, you've reached the home of Chris and Hazel Richardson. We're not in right now, so leave a message after the tone, and we'll get back to you as soon as we can."

Then, the beep.

Click-clack, click-clack.

The scuttling intensified, almost drowning out the recording.

"Hi, Isobel, are you there...? Izzy? Chris, she's not answering."

"Maybe she's in the bathroom?"

The Richardsons. Why the hell were they phoning? They should be on their way home!

"Isobel? If you're there, pick up, please."

"Just leave the damn message."

"Would you be quiet? I'm trying to. Isobel, if you can hear me, this is Mrs Richardson. We've had engine trouble, and we're at a service station getting it fixed. I'm really sorry, but we're gonna be home late, probably after twelve."

"Definitely after twelve."

"Would you shut up? Sorry, Izzy, not you. My husband is being a... listen, I hope you're okay to stay a little longer. We'll pay you overtime, of course, and you can help yourself to anything in the—"

Another beep, cutting the message off.

Isobel slid down the wall, tears flooding her eyes. She couldn't wait that long.

Click-clack, click-clack.

Florence stirred in her bed.

Don't wake up!

She had to reach the phone and call the police... but not until it was safe to do so. And so she waited, watching the seconds tick by on the clock. Fifteen minutes passed, then half-an-hour, and in that time, she heard neither a click nor a clack. The monsters were either gone... or waiting patiently.

Turning the door handle, Isobel peered through the gap.

The house was deathly silent.

She opened the door wider and took an uncertain step

into the hallway. The board groaned tiredly beneath her foot.

Easy does it...

Keeping low, she tip-toed towards the stairs. From there, she crouched and looked at the wooden table near the foot of the stairs, upon which sat a white push-button phone. She wouldn't even have to go all the way down; it was reachable through the rails about five steps from the bottom.

Every instinct told her to return to the bedroom, but James could still be alive out there, and who knew when the Richardsons would be home? If the monsters realised she and Florence were up here, they'd find a way in, much like they had with Phil McFarlane, murdered in his own home only two nights prior. Her boyfriend had been first on the scene, and when he told her the way Phil's blood had dripped from the ceiling—

Stop thinking about it.

She needed to reach that phone.

Nothing moved in the house as Isobel made her way down. Her eyes darted from door to door.

Almost there.

A step creaked, and she winced, waiting for the creatures to pounce. When they didn't, she resumed her journey.

As long as you don't see them, she thought, *you'll be okay. No one who sees them lives.*

Isobel was halfway down the stairs when Florence whimpered in her bedroom. Her body tensed.

Don't wake up, don't wake up.

She wished James was here.

Why? They already got him.

Tears nipped at her eyes, and she blinked them away. This was no time to cry. The phone was close. She reached between the rails, but she wasn't quite there yet. Two more steps should do it.

She took them painstakingly slowly, every subtle creak and groan a dagger in her heart.

Made it.

Isobel pressed up against the rail, stretching her arm through and groping for the receiver. Her fingertips brushed the plastic, and—

The phone rang again.

This time, Isobel had to scream. There was no physical way to hold it in.

Click-clack, click-clack.

She shot her hand back through. The phone acted like a siren, the grating screech a clarion call echoing throughout the house.

Click-clack, click-clack.

Motion along the hallway, long legs scurrying rapidly.

She ran up the stairs, the monsters in pursuit. One skidded into the downstairs hallway and knocked into the phone table, sending it crashing to the floor. The ringing stopped, but Isobel never slowed.

Click-clack, click-clack.

They were on the stairs.

"Florence!" she yelled. "Wake up!"

She crashed through the door and into the child's bedroom, slamming it behind her. Florence was awake, her eyes wide with fear and surprise, but Isobel would deal with her later. She ran to the chest of drawers and dragged it in front of the door.

Something smacked against the other side.

Florence squealed as the chest shifted several inches, scraping along the carpet. It wouldn't hold. Isobel looked around the room.

The wardrobe.

It was old, and heavy, and she didn't know if she could move it. She put her shoulder against the wood and pushed. "Help me!"

Florence leapt from the bed and tried her best. The monster hit the door again, opening it further. Thin, spider-like legs reached through, the wall glowing an obscene pink.

With a guttural yell, Isobel crouched and hooked her fingers under the wardrobe, lifting it, *tipping* it, adrenaline surging through her veins. "Come on!" she cried, raising the wardrobe until gravity took over. It crashed against the chest of drawers, the doors opening and disgorging clothes and toys like disembowelled guts.

That would hold them... but for how long? She couldn't think with Florence screaming.

"I want my mummy!" wailed the little girl.

"Everything's going to be alright," Isobel said in her calmest voice. "I need you to be very brave and put on your dressing gown. We're going outside."

Thump! Thump thump!

The impacts came in quick succession. There were more than one monster. The wardrobe was firm, but—

Crack!

The wooden door splintered.

It wouldn't last. Isobel looked at Florence. The little girl was still on the bed in her nightgown.

"Fuck!"

She ran to the window and fumbled the latch, opening it as wide as it would go. She checked the drop. Twenty feet?

It was their only chance.

She snatched Florence up in her arms. How to do this? Dangle her out and let her fall? No, the distance was too great for her young bones.

Crack!

Isobel turned to the door. Monsters flitted back and forth behind broken panels, long, muscular arms and skeletal legs scratching at the wood.

She gripped Florence in a hug and put one leg over the ledge, searching desperately for a foothold. "Don't let go of me!"

Smash!

A chunk of wood flew from the door.

Isobel kicked off the wall, launching her and Florence out the window. She hoped to land on both feet.

She failed.

One foot hit the ground first, her ankle breaking instantly. Her head struck the paving slab, pain erupting as her brain collided with her skull. Unharmed, Florence squirmed free and looked up at the window. She pointed and shrieked.

Eight legs spread out from the frame like a dead flower blossoming back into life. They gripped onto the stone wall, and the nightmarish, fleshy body emerged.

"The car!" screamed Isobel from her prone position. "Get to the police car!"

Florence didn't move. She stood stock still in the pouring rain as the huge *thing* advanced. Isobel forced herself to rise. She grabbed Florence by the scruff of her nightgown and shoved her towards the car.

"The door's open!" She hobbled after the toddler. "Get inside!"

Click-clack, click-clack.

It scuttled down the wall.

Florence stood by the car, her little hand reaching for the handle.

"Go! *Get in!*"

Florence managed to open the door and climb inside. She pulled it shut, and as Isobel staggered onwards through the pouring rain, dragging her broken ankle, she watched as the little girl pressed the door locks down into place.

"No! Wait for me!" She reached the car and rattled the handle. "Florence! Open up!" The toddler sat in the driver's seat, hugging her knees to her chest. "Florence, please! I can drive us out of—"

The monster struck Isobel, knocking her to the ground, and as she lay there, the colossal black shape blotting out the sky, she was reminded of the time that car had hit her. She had been eight years old, and despite the vehicle only travelling at twenty miles per hour, the resulting impact had shattered her leg. Endless rounds of surgery and several steel rods enabled her to walk again, but nothing could be done about her pronounced limp.

Her schoolmates had teased her mercilessly, until eventually Isobel discovered that the best way to deal with bullies was to become one herself. The 'tough bitch' persona she developed had carried her through high school, though she took no pleasure in her actions. Oftentimes, she cried herself to sleep over her treatment of others, aware of how pitiful she truly was.

Now, close to death, she recalled the immediate aftermath of the accident, lying flat on her back and staring up at the rusted, steaming undercarriage of the car. But the pain she had felt that day, and the emotional turmoil over the ensuing years, had nothing on this raw horror.

The monster mounted her, and a puckered pink orifice quivered above her face.

"No," she sobbed, as the hole flexed and spurted thick green fluid over her. She covered her face with her hands, but the liquid burned like acid. Her skin withered away, the flesh dissolving in runny lumps. More of the vile fluid seeped onto her chest and stomach, and she screamed as her flesh melted, layers of peeling skin sliding off her skull and splatting to the ground in a putrid, bloody soup. Only when her own tongue liquefied in her mouth did the screaming stop.

But not the pain.

For the creatures feasted on Isobel for a long, long time, abandoning her only when sirens wailed in the distance and the Auchenmullan police force, alerted by Florence's concerned mother, pulled up outside the house. What PC Lawrence Carlisle found upon arrival was a *new* kind of monster lying on the gravel, one in the approximate size and shape of a young girl in the prime of her life.

And as Isobel Macleod mercifully slipped away, the last thing she heard was PC Carlisle saying, "Jesus Christ, what the fuck is *that*?"

She would have wept if she still had a face.

PART III

25

———

On Sunday, Sammo paid them a visit.

Lucy spotted him wandering between the scarecrows sometime before lunch, and when she called his name, he gambolled over and rolled onto his back, ready to be tickled.

"Where have you been?" she asked, hugging his round body and blowing raspberries on his belly. "I tried to introduce you to Rab, but when you weren't there, he didn't believe me! Not that it mattered," she added proudly. "We still kissed." She sat and leaned against her friend. "Oh, Sammo, it was amazing! You should meet him. I think you'd like each other."

She called her dad down from his office by shouting up at the window, and he appeared moments later with a football under his arm, saying, "Found this in a cupboard. Reckon he'll want to play?"

He dribbled the ball towards Sammo and kicked it at the monster. The football bopped him on the snout and landed between his legs.

Sammo grunted.

"You're supposed to kick it back," Lucy told him. "Like

this!" She picked up the ball and drop-kicked it to her father. That was the plan, anyway. The ball careened off to the side and hit the barn. Her dad gave chase — it was the first time she'd seen him run in about ten years — and hoofed the ball back to her. This continued for some time, until at last Sammo tried to join in. The monster reached for the ball, but his claws were too sharp, and they punctured the leather, deflating it.

Lucy wondered if it was deliberate.

Regardless, the game was over, so she and Sammo retreated to the barn to catch-up while her dad returned to the farmhouse. He claimed it was to do some writing, but judging by his wheezing, and the way he clutched his chest, Lucy thought he was going for a nap.

Later that afternoon, he drove them to Auchenmullan to pick up supplies for dinner. His second date with Miss Wade loomed, and this time he wanted Lucy to eat with them at the table. It was easy for him to say, because he wasn't the one making the damn dinner.

Turned out it wasn't so bad.

They played a bunch of games the previous occupants had left behind; *Scrabble* and *Uno,* and then *Dream Phone,* which amused Lucy no end, especially when her dad ended up with hunky Spencer. Then they ate, and Lucy was allowed another small glass of wine, which she drank while dodging questions about Rab, who her dad jokingly referred to as 'her boyfriend.' Lucy responded by asking Miss Wade if 'dad's girlfriend' had enjoyed her meal, which promptly shut him up.

After dinner, she invited Miss Wade to meet Sammo properly, and they headed off to the barn, leaving her dad in the kitchen to load the dishwasher.

"How are you getting on in Helsbridge?" asked Miss

Wade, as they petted Sammo and fed him branches. "Settling in well?"

"You mean apart from all the monsters trying to kill me?"

"Yeah." Miss Wade's expression turned grim. "Apart from that."

"In that case, I'm settling in fine, thanks."

"Anyone bothering you at school?"

"Nope. Well, one girl was, but we've made up, I think."

Miss Wade brightened. "Glad to hear it. I found Auchenmullan pretty off-putting when I first arrived. I wouldn't say they shunned me in the streets, but if they did talk to me, all they asked was if I had a boyfriend or a husband, and if I was thinking of having children. They only warmed up when I convinced them that, as someone who spends all day around kids, the last thing I wanted was to come home to more of them." She touched Lucy's shoulder. "No offence."

"None taken. I'm more of an adult, anyway."

"That you are, Lucy."

Sammo groaned, and used his paw to move Miss Wade's hand from Lucy's shoulder back to his belly.

"I also wanted to apologise again for the other morning," her teacher said. "That was very unprofessional of me."

"That's okay. You saw me in my underwear the night before, so I guess that makes us even." She looked out at the field. "It's getting dark. We should head in soon."

"Yeah, you're right," said Miss Wade. "One more branch for Sammo, and then we'll go. It's nice to get some girl time, isn't it?"

"It is. Sammo's fun to talk to, but he mostly grunts." She patted the monster's belly. "Don't you, Sammo? You're not a big talker!"

Lucy watched Miss Wade out of the corner of her eye.

The woman was staring off into the distance like she had something on her mind.

"You like my dad, don't you?"

"I think he's a great guy."

"He's okay. He's been sad for a long time. We both have. But you make him happy, and he's much easier to live with when he's happy. Otherwise, he just wants to talk to *me* all day, and who's got time for that?"

Miss Wade smiled. "He makes me happy, too. And that's kinda what I wanted to talk to you about. Between you and me — and bear in mind, I haven't discussed this with your dad yet, because I wanted to see how you felt about it first — but I was thinking that maybe... that, y'know, it might be a good idea if..."

"What are you trying to say? You can tell me, I can usually keep a secret."

"Usually?"

"Depends how good the gossip is."

The smile dropped from Miss Wade's face. "Lucy, it's not safe here. We both know that. And I also know we've just met, but still... I thought that, maybe, you and your dad could stay at my place in Auchenmullan for a while? Just until he's back on his feet. It doesn't mean anything, but I'd sleep better knowing you two were far from Helsbridge... and from these woods."

"Huh," said Lucy.

"You can mull it over. I have a big house, and there's a lot more to Auchenmullan than Helsbridge. There's a bowling alley and shops, and the people there don't talk about monsters all day. Well, not all of them."

"Do you have a TV?"

"I have two."

"I see. And could I have one in my room?"

"Of course," laughed Miss Wade.

Lucy nodded, and clapped her hands together. "Okay... so when can we move?"

~

Miss Wade went in first, leaving Lucy — under strict instructions to be home in the next five minutes — in the barn with Sammo.

"You heard Miss Wade," she said to her friend, as she stroked his fur, "though I don't know if you understand her like you understand me. Basically, we're gonna be moving away for a while. But I promise it won't be forever, and we'll come back and see you all the time."

Sammo grunted. He was wearing the deflated football as a hat, and she found it hard to take him seriously.

"It's because of the monsters," she said. "I know we're friends — *best* friends — but you have a job, and I'm a distraction. What you do, Sammo... it's brave. You protect us, don't you? All of us. Even the jerks." She stood, and picked up one of his sticks. "And for that, on behalf of the people of Helsbridge," — she rested the stick on his shoulder — "I dub you Sir Sammo of Brannigan, Guardian of the Forest and Friend of Lucy."

Sammo responded by taking the stick in his mouth and chewing on it.

"I'm trying to knight you, Sammo! Don't eat the ceremonial sword."

Too late. He stripped the branch bare and tossed it aside. She stared at him with love in her heart, and kissed him on the cheek. "It'll be dark soon. I'd better—"

His ears shot up, alert and listening.

"What is it?" She ran to the door. "Do you hear them?"

But it wasn't the monsters.

Not this time.

Lights flitted through the trees like phantoms, accompanied by the quiet fury of distant, roaring engines. Cars. More than one. Hell, even *one* was one too many. They had no business here.

Sammo joined her at the door. She scratched behind his ear and pointed to the forest.

"Go," she said, her heart racing. "Get out of here."

For Lucy was sure of one thing, and one thing only.

The people in the cars were coming for *him*.

26

SAMMO REMAINED ROOTED TO THE SPOT.

"Go, *now!*" she urged. Why wouldn't he budge? She looked down at his paws, at the talon-like claws protruding from the thick clumps of fur.

He wanted to protect her.

"I can handle myself," she said. "It's not me they want, Sammo. It's you!"

He gazed at her with glassy eyes.

The engines grew louder.

"Sammo, please. Go somewhere safe. For a little while. When we go to stay with Miss Wade, we'll switch the scarecrows off, and when we come back to see you, I'll put them on again so you know I'm back, okay? *Okay?*"

If only she knew he understood her. If only he could talk!

"Please, Sammo. I love you, but you have to go!" Tears streamed down her cheeks. Had she done nothing but cry since she arrived? It seemed that way. Her friend lumbered towards the door, and looked back at her.

"I won't let them find you, Sammo. Never."

He stared at her a moment longer, then took off into the forest.

"Run," she whispered. "Run and hide."

A procession of cars and SUVs emerged into the clearing. Lucy scurried through the long grass to the bathroom window at the rear of the building. Her dad had left it open for Miss Wade's visit, and it would allow her access without being seen.

She arrived at the window. It wasn't high, but she was short, and had to stand on a rusted metal bucket to reach the frame and haul herself up. Without pausing to consider whether someone might be using the toilet — thankfully, no one was — she clambered through the window and over the cistern, jumping down onto the linoleum floor. Music played from the living room, and she ran to the door and barged her way in.

"Dad!" she shouted.

They were canoodling on the couch.

"Mhhhm!" her dad said, his lips locked around Miss Wade's.

"Oh shit, Lucy, learn to knock!" said the teacher, as she pulled away.

"There are people outside," she panted. "Lots of them, in cars!"

The adults looked at each other, and then her dad was on his feet and heading to the window. He hauled back the curtains.

"She's not wrong," he said flatly. "That is a lot of cars."

Miss Wade joined him. "That's a lot of *people.*" She failed to hide the unease in her voice.

"What do they want?" asked Lucy.

Her dad stared at Miss Wade. "Are parent-teacher relationships forbidden?"

"I mean, they're frowned upon... but no one knows about us."

Lucy kept quiet. She *had* told Rab about them, but she trusted him. After all, they had shared a kiss, and one day, maybe more.

Her dad cleared his throat. "Guess I should go out and talk to them."

"No, don't!" said Lucy. She tugged on his arm. "Let's escape out the back."

"And go where? You're being silly. I'm sure it's a misunderstanding."

Only Miss Wade remained at the window. "Brian," she said, the colour draining from her face. "They've got guns."

"Guns? How have they got guns?"

"They're farmers. They use them to protect their livestock."

"Yeah, but why are they bringing them *here?*"

Lucy listened, silently trembling. She waited for a knock at the door. It never came. Rather, the front door flew open from a violent kick. She screamed and clung to her dad.

"Elli," he said. "Take Lucy, and go upstairs."

"I'm not leaving you," they said at the same time.

A ruddy-faced man in a checked shirt and flat-cap was first to enter. Tucked under his arm was a double-barrelled shotgun.

"Who are you?" her dad asked in the most authoritative tone she had ever heard him use. "And what the hell are you doing in my house?"

The man didn't answer. He took the shotgun in his hands and held it at waist height as more men and women filtered in carrying shotguns and rifles. The hallway filled up, yet still more entered, forcing Lucy and the two adults into the living room.

In the background, her dad's jazz music played on. Even Lucy was familiar with the gravelly tones of Louis Armstrong.

"Get out of my house," her dad barked at the intruders. "Get the fuck out—"

A farmer stepped forwards like an unelected leader. "Where is it? Where's the monster?"

Lucy peered out from behind her dad. There must have been a dozen people in the room with them, and many more in the hall. Men, women, even some children.

"I don't know what you're talking about," her dad said. "There's been a mistake."

"We know your daughter's hiding it!" shrieked a woman. "It needs to die before it kills again!"

"Are you people insane?" her dad shouted over the racket.

"Brian," said Miss Wade, "Don't antagonise them." She stepped forwards. "Folks, my name is Elli Wade. I recognise some of you, and I'm sure some of you recognise me. I teach art at Kingussie High School, and—"

A woman spat in her face, silencing her. "Shut up, you whore," she said.

"If you knew about this monster," another woman piped up, "then you're as guilty as *they* are." She pointed at Lucy and her dad. "You're complicit in the deaths of our children!"

Unflustered, Miss Wade wiped the spit from her face. "No one is complicit in anything. Now, why don't we all sit down and talk, and try to figure out—"

This time, the woman slapped her. Lucy's dad marched angrily forwards, and two shotgun barrels jabbed into his ribs.

"I wouldnae take another step," said the farmer on the

other end of the gun. "Unless you want tae make your wee lassie an orphan."

"Guys, this is crazy!" her dad said.

"Tell us where it is," said the farmer, his brow creasing. "Show us where you're hiding the monster that steals our children."

"We don't have a monster. You can check all you want, you won't find anything."

"She keeps it in the barn."

Lucy recognised the voice. She felt sick.

"What's that, lad? Speak up!" said a bald man in horn-rimmed glasses.

A pale, skinny boy was ushered to the front of the group.

"In the barn," said Rab, his eyes glassy behind his spectacles. He pointed at Lucy. "That's where she keeps the monster that killed my sister."

Lucy's stomach dropped. Isobel was dead? How? When?

"Wait a minute!" Her dad struggled to be heard over the raised, angry voices. "You don't understand. We *had* a monster, but it's not—"

"He admits it!"

"He's guilty!"

"They all are! String 'em up!"

"Stop, stop!" her dad yelled. "Listen to me, please! He was friendly! He's not the one you're looking for!"

Lucy glanced around for a way out. Short of breaking through a window, there was no escape.

"Take us to the barn," someone said.

"He's not there anymore!" Lucy shouted. All eyes turned to her. "He... he was there for a while, but he's gone now."

The farmer trained the shotgun on her. "Gone where? Speak, child!"

She stared at the barrel. Was it loaded? Would he shoot?

"Gone where?"

"Back home," she stuttered. She had never even *seen* a gun before, never mind had one aimed at her. "Back to his nest."

"Take us there," the man said.

"But he's nice," she said. It came out as a sob. "He's my friend."

Lucy lowered her gaze as the voices descended into a confusing jumble of demands and accusations.

"Take us to him..."

"He killed my Isobel..."

"Get that gun away from my daughter..."

"Check the barn..."

"Mrs Riley, I teach your son..."

"Kill them..."

"She knows where it lives..."

"She's a liar..."

"Listen to yourselves!"

"Kill the monster, then kill them all..."

"He's never hurt anyone..."

"Tonight, it dies..."

"He protects us..."

Lucy clamped her hands over her ears to shut out the noise. The townsfolk shouted over each other, shrieking threats as her dad and Miss Wade tried in vain to placate them. These people were worse than the monsters. Worse, because they were human, and should know better. They had the capacity for reason, for change, for understanding.

So why wouldn't they listen?

Someone grabbed her arm. She looked up into the contorted face of a middle-aged man, his eyes sunken, cheeks sallow. He yanked her into the crowd, and she reached for her dad. He came for her, but one man struck him across the head with the butt of his rifle, and he fell.

"Dad!"

The man held her shoulders and marched her through the crowd. Some hit her as she passed, while others spat on her and slapped the back of her head. She looked at Rab, begging, *pleading*.

Unable to meet her gaze, he simply turned away.

"Where's my daughter?" she heard her dad shout, before they shoved her through the front door and out onto the grass. She tried to run, and a woman yanked her back by her hair and pushed her in the direction of the barn. They paraded her onwards, braying and bellowing, and each time she turned to look for her dad, they smacked her across her head.

"He's not here," she wept, stumbling towards the barn as the dead-eyed scarecrows looked on impassively. They neared the entrance. Three men, armed and ready, entered the dilapidated building. The rest hung back in anticipation.

Minutes ticked by. Lucy's dad caught up to her, his shirt

collar stained with blood, his arm slung over Miss Wade's shoulder.

The men exited the barn.

"There's nothing in there now," one said. "But there's weird black shite everywhere. Must be monster blood."

She almost told them they were correct — it *was* monster blood, but not Sammo's — then decided against it.

Their minds were made up.

"Where's it gone?" someone growled. "Take us to it!"

"Let me handle this," her dad said, positioning himself between Lucy and the mob. He raised his hands. "Okay, you win. If you promise to leave us alone, we'll take you there."

"No, dad!" she shouted.

He turned to her. "Lucy, we've no fucking choice."

"But they'll *kill* him."

"They'll kill *us*," he hissed. "Don't you understand that?"

She looked to Miss Wade.

Her teacher stepped forwards. "She's just a child," she said to the crowd. "Look at yourselves! You're pointing guns at a child!"

"Whether she knows it or not," came the retort, "she's in league with the devil!"

"That is no *devil*," said Miss Wade. She lowered her voice. "Please, she's telling the truth. There *are* different monsters out there, and this one — the one Lucy befriended — was no killer. I met him. All three of us did, and we're still standing here, aren't we? We're not dead! Come on, I *know* you're reasonable people. I recognise most of you from parents' evenings, for christ's sake. Let's just be civilised and—"

A gun went off.

Everything after that seemed to happen in slow-motion.

Miss Wade's stomach exploded with a thunderous roar,

blood spraying in a crimson eruption, chunks of flesh and slivers of splintered bone raining down around her in a miserable shower of gore. She took one faltering step backwards, instinctively clasping her hand across her belly in a feeble attempt to prevent her intestines from slopping out of the wound, and crumpled to the ground.

Frozen in place, Lucy watched her father drop to his knees beside Miss Wade. He didn't cry out, or scream. It was nothing like the movies. He just cradled the woman's head as blood spilled over her delicate chin. Her leg spasmed, violently kicking out at nothing.

And then, Lucy watched the woman draw her final breath.

They all did.

The man who had shot her... the crowd of blood-crazed townspeople... their children... even the scarecrows... they *all* stood idly by and watched as Miss Wade died.

27

———

Nobody moved. The townsfolk cast their eyes down, murmuring amongst themselves about how it was 'unavoidable,' and that Miss Wade had 'brought it on herself.'

"An outsider wouldn't understand," one of them whispered to vague rumbles of agreement.

Lucy turned away from the grisly spectacle and vomited, retching until there was nothing left inside her.

"She's dead," her dad was mumbling. "You killed her."

On weak knees, Lucy staggered over to him and laid her hand on his shoulder. He looked up at her with haunted eyes.

"Take them to Sammo," he said hollowly. "Show them where their goddam monster lives."

"No," she said.

"Just... *do it.*" He looked down at Miss Wade, her guts steaming on the grass. "Do it for Elli."

"Don't say that." Her limp hand slid from his shoulder. "That's not fair."

"Life's unfair," he said calmly. "Haven't you realised that yet? It gives you everything, then takes it all away."

"I won't do it."

"You have to. It's time to grow up, Lucy." He stroked his fingers down Miss Wade's face. "Your stubbornness has already cost one life. Don't make it cost two more."

"You don't mean that," she said. "You can't believe that."

One of the men strode forwards. "Awright, that's enough." He aimed the barrel at Lucy. "Lead the way."

She looked to her dad for help, and — like Rab before him — he turned away. Reeling from his accusation, she stumbled dazedly towards the forest. Quieter than before, the group followed close behind.

Your stubbornness has already cost one life.

Lucy cried. Was she responsible?

Don't make it cost two more.

As she reached the trees, she checked her dad was following.

He was.

Why did he refuse to help? He, of all people, should understand that if Sammo were to die, the consequences would be disastrous. The monsters would run riot. Or what if he chose to defend himself against the mob? He could rip them to shreds with his claws.

But he wouldn't. It wasn't in Sammo's nature. His heart was purer than that of any human.

He was better than all of them.

On she walked, numb and unfeeling. She realised she didn't need her father. She didn't need anyone, not anymore.

Life's unfair.

Was it true? Or just what people who'd stopped dreaming told themselves? She pictured Miss Wade lying in her father's arms, and hesitated, unsure if she could go on.

The barrel of a gun jabbed into her spine. *"Keep moving."*

She did. Onwards through the forest she trudged, until

they came to the old monuments. There, she waited as the townsfolk stopped to inspect the writing carved into the stones.

"Whit devilry is this?" one man asked.

"It's Gaelic," a woman said. "Rory, can you read it?"

Using his rifle as a walking stick, a white-haired man stepped forwards and stood before the monument. He retrieved glasses from his pocket and balanced them on his nose, squinting at the words.

"Seachad air a' phuing so tha cunnart," he said gravely, and turned to the others. "It's a warning. Roughly, it means, *beyond this point, there is danger.*"

"Aye," someone said. "Nae shite."

Troubled, the townsfolk looked at each other, as if debating whether to continue. At first, Lucy was surprised they hadn't encountered the monuments before. But why would they have? They knew better than to venture into the woods, the ancient wisdom doubtlessly passed down from generation to generation. Hell, Rab had said it himself; no one in town even knew what the monsters looked like.

"I say we keep going," the older man growled. "If anyone wishes to turn back, I winnae stop you. But we're aw here together, and there's strength in numbers. This may be our only chance to put an end tae centuries of misery for this godforsaken region."

No one dared move. Lucy hoped they they would give up, but without another word, the older man shoved her forwards and resumed walking. Like a plague of mindless lemmings, the others followed, their footsteps crunching through the undergrowth.

There was no going back now.

Lucy walked on, leaving the dire warnings behind, passing the loch where Sammo had brought her after the first near-death encounter. Trees blanked out the sun, her shoes squelching in thick, muddy pools. She didn't even know where she was going, yet when she found herself standing before a tall tree with lush, golden foliage, she knew that, somehow, they had arrived at Sammo's nest.

Walk on.

And then what? Perhaps her dad was right. Life had gifted her a new beginning, new friends, and a caring father who loved her... and then taken it all away in a heartbeat. All that remained was Sammo. Without him, she would have nothing left to lose. And maybe that was what growing up was all about? Accepting that you'll never be happy, secure in the knowledge that there's nothing left for life to take from you.

She looked at the mob's angry faces. The hike had not dulled their rage.

Words failed her, so she motioned to the tree and sat cross-legged on the forest floor.

Her father came to her and stood by her side. "You did the right thing," he muttered. "We're gonna get through this."

"Yeah," she said, though deep down, she knew — and suspected he did too — that after tonight, nothing would ever be the same again.

28

———

THE TOWNSFOLK FORMED A SEMI-CIRCLE, GAZING IN AWE AT the mighty tree before getting to work. The adults ritually stripped the bark from the lower trunk, while the children gathered twigs and branches and stacked them around the base as kindling.

Lucy sat helplessly, chewing her nails as panic mounted.

"Where's Norman?" one of the farmers asked. "We need the agricultural burner."

The what?

"Right here, mate," said Norman, a thickset man in a parka with a metal canister strapped to his back. Lucy knew what he was carrying. She had rented *The Thing* on video last year, and recognised the device.

An agricultural burner was a fancy name for a fucking *flamethrower*.

"No," she whimpered involuntarily.

"You bring spare fuel?" someone asked.

"Aye. Want it? *Danny, come here!*"

A teenage boy appeared carrying another canister, the liquid sloshing around inside. He lugged it to the base of the tree and unscrewed the cap, permeating the air with the suffocating stench of gasoline.

One man hacked grooves into the trunk with a hand-axe, then stepped back to allow the boy with the canister to pour the gasoline into them. The remaining fuel was emptied over the firewood, the townsfolk retreating to a safe distance as Norman approached the tree, a small blue flame sparking from the tip of his flamethrower.

He paused only once, when, high above, the monster roared. Lucy knew it to be a howl of despair, but the townspeople took it as a sign of imminent danger.

"Burn it, Norman! Burn it to the fucking ground!"

"They're going to kill him," Lucy mumbled to herself.

Her dad must have overheard, for he said, "It's for the best."

Whoosh!

The dark woods fleetingly illuminated as Norman blasted a ball of pure, devastating fire into the air.

"Ready?" he called.

The crowd cheered — they fucking *cheered* — and Norman turned to the kindling.

"Don't do it," moaned Lucy, her voice lost amid the expectant cries.

Too late.

Flames shot from the nozzle. The fire crackled and spat, then roared as the gasoline ignited, engulfing the pyre in a massive conflagration.

From high up, Sammo bellowed, and the people stepped back in fear.

"Burn!" one of the men shouted. "Let the cleansing fire burn this monstrosity from existence!"

"What about them?" a woman in a shell-suit asked, directing her ire at Lucy and her dad. "They're part of this!"

"My daughter would still be alive if it wasn't for her!" another shouted. From the way the woman clung to Rab, Lucy assumed she was Isobel's mum. She tried to summon some sympathy for Rab and his family, and found none.

Her dad raised his hands. "We brought you here. Let us go, and you'll never see us again."

She wondered if he meant it. Would he honestly let Miss Wade's killers go unpunished?

An old man, leaning heavily on a stick, shook his head. *"They know too much,"* he said.

Despite the intensity of the roaring fire, the words sent a chill down Lucy's spine. They wouldn't do it, would they? After forcing her to betray Sammo... they wouldn't kill them?

Golden leaves rained down like snowfall at sunset, twinkling in the fiery glow. Lucy looked up at the tree, at the branches that shook and trembled.

"No!" she screamed. He was coming down. *"Run!"*

The mob followed her gaze, tilting their heads — and firearms — upwards in dreadful anticipation. The foliage parted to reveal Sammo's blank, adorable face... and they shrieked in terror.

"He's friendly," cried Lucy. She got to her feet, tugging on the sleeves of the townsfolk. "Can't you see that? *He's friendly!*"

He descended further, recoiling at the ferocious heat that burned his tree from the inside, killing it. His expressionless eyes looked at Lucy.

"I'm sorry," she said, and broke down. "They made me."

He seemed to nod in acknowledgement — or so she imagined — and that was when the men opened fire.

The first shot caught Sammo on his side. He uttered a cry, losing his grip on the tree and crashing headfirst to the forest floor, narrowly missing the inferno. He tucked his head before impact, landing in a crude forward roll.

"No!" screamed Lucy.

The men advanced, and she ran for Sammo, throwing herself in front of him and spreading her arms and legs wide.

"Don't shoot him!"

"Get out of the way," a farmer said, with the cold, merciless voice of a soldier.

"He didn't do anything! He's never hurt anyone. Look at him! He could kill you all if he wanted to!"

Rab stepped forwards, the churning blaze reflected in his glasses. For the first time that evening, he dared to look her in the eyes. "Move," he said coldly. "Or they'll shoot you too."

"Please," she begged, looking to each of the adults in turn. Their stony faces regarded her uncaringly, anger and hatred seething behind dead eyes. She thought of what they had done to Miss Wade, and how none cared that they had cut down an innocent woman for the crime of protecting her friends.

Innocent didn't mean much, these days.

A gun fired. The ground in front of Lucy exploded in a puff of dirt and pine needles.

"Last warning," the farmer sneered. "Or so help me God, I'll..."

"Then do it." She glared at him. "Kill me, you fucking—"

Someone grabbed her from behind. One arm closed around her waist and lifted her off her feet, while a hand clamped over her mouth. She kicked, her heels making firm contact, but her attacker wrapped her in a tight bearhug, carrying her away and wrestling her to the ground. She managed to turn, and stared into the face of her father.

"Get off me!" she screamed, but the deafening roar of gunfire drowned out her frantic words.

The killing had begun.

The men fired indiscriminately. Sammo tried to run, but the bullets and shells punctured his flesh with audible pops. Blood spurted from the entry wounds as the projectiles buried themselves deep in his flesh. Lucy attempted to wriggle out from under her father, but he pressed her down into the mud.

"It's him or us!" he cried. *"Him or us!"*

Sammo curled into a protective ball as more shots slammed into him. His fur split in dozens of places, exposing pink tissue and bloody muscle. He roared, dragging himself through the mud, but the men kept firing, bullet holes peppering his hairy body until he slumped onto his belly.

Then it was the turn of the children. They crowded Sammo, kicking him and smacking him with sticks.

Once more, Lucy tried to slither free from her dad's clutches, but he held her down.

Sammo lay still. His chest slowly — oh, so slowly — rose... and then fell. Only the crackle of the fire sounded, the flames licking higher as they effortlessly scaled the trunk, charring it black.

Then, Sammo cried out. The heartbreaking sound echoed throughout the forest, and Lucy knew he was dying.

"Bring out the lad," a farmer said, and the mob parted for Rab and his mother. Silently, they walked hand-in-hand towards Sammo, the mother clutching an axe. They stopped by his body, and the woman dipped her fingers into Sammo's wounds.

He didn't react.

Rab's mother painted crude markings on the boy's

cheeks and forehead with her bloodstained fingertips. Then, she handed him the axe.

"Finish it," she said. "For Isobel."

Rab stared at the weapon, gripping it in both hands.

"Don't," sobbed Lucy.

He turned to her with tears in his eyes. "It killed my sister."

"It wasn't him, Rab. I swear it wasn't. Please, let him live!"

Rab looked down at the shivering mass of bloodied fur. "It's a mercy killing," he said.

"If you do it," said Lucy, "I'll fucking kill you."

Rab shrugged with weary resignation, and turned to Sammo. "You bastard," he snarled, and raised the axe above his—

Click-clack, click-clack.

The weapon hung in the air. Rab looked to his mother.

Click-clack, click-clack.

"My god," someone said.

Lucy's father released her, and she scrambled to her feet. "We have to go," she said to him, wiping her eyes with her sleeve. "Now."

He didn't move.

No one did.

Click-clack, click-clack, click-clack, click-clack, click-clack, click-clack, click-clack, click-clack, click-clack, click-clack, click-clack, CLICK-CLACK CLICK-CLACK CLICK-CLACK.

She punched his arm. "Come on!"

A few men hurriedly reloaded their weapons. They glanced at each other in confusion.

"I thought..."

"But..."

"We killed it..."

For the last time, Lucy looked at Sammo.

"I'm sorry," she whispered, and thought she saw a glint of understanding in his eyes. "I love you, my friend."

He raised one paw off the ground, and licked his bloody tongue across his snout.

The paw fell limp.

Click-clack, click-clack.

Around her, some of the townsfolk started to run. The children dropped their sticks, cowering behind their parents, for they all knew that sound. Everyone in Helsbridge did.

Click-clack, click-clack.

The harbinger of death.

Someone screamed. No, not someone, some *thing*. More followed, from all around, the forest alive with bloodcurdling, inhuman wails.

Lucy grabbed her dad's arm and tugged him towards her, snapping him from his stupor. He looked at her in sheer terror.

"Run," she said.

29

———

THE FIRST MONSTER SPRANG OUT OF THE DARKNESS, LANDING on the closest farmer. He tried to wrestle his gun free, but fleshy pincers closed around his neck and sliced deep. His arteries ejected blood at high velocity, the man gurgling in anguish as more creatures emerged through the thick, Stygian smoke.

The tree was ablaze now.

It lit up the forest, and in the fraction of a second before Lucy and her father ran, she cast a single worried glance over her shoulder at the approaching monsters.

There were hundreds of them.

Fucking *hundreds*.

They scrambled over each other in a wave of chaotic bedlam, their limbs tangling, vile sacs puffing up in a shimmering pink luminescence.

Then she was off, hurtling through the forest, her father by her side. The monsters rampaged through the undergrowth, as the foolhardy souls who remained behind opened fire. The useless gunshots rang out like whip cracks, before the thunderous clicking of wasted, monstrous limbs gobbled them up.

With Sammo gone, there was no one left to protect them.

As Lucy ran, she heard the yelps and cries of the stragglers. She looked back at the swarming darkness as it engulfed a young boy, cutting his screams short.

A shotgun blast rang out.

It was close to Lucy, and her ears rang. A man in front of her stood with the weapon held to his shoulder, firing off blasts into the seething mass.

"Careful!" Lucy's father shouted, and a woman howled as a stray shot hit her. She dropped, and with blood streaming down her chest, she opened her mouth to scream. Before she could, the monsters descended on her in a flesh-tearing frenzy, slashing and tearing at her defenceless body.

Lucy kept running. A cold emptiness had settled in her gut, and she felt nothing much of anything. Let those fools try to fight; for every person that died helped thin the stampeding herd.

On she ran, through mud and ferns and grasping limbs, her head down, dodging roots and trees until the clicking softened, and the screams faded. Only then did Lucy dare to look.

Behind her, the forest was quiet.

Where had the monsters gone? Had they halted to feast on the ragged flesh of the fallen? Or changed direction and headed towards Helsbridge? The town was unprotected now. If they wanted to, the monstrous hellspawn could—

"Lucy, come on!" her father shouted.

She saw the clearing, yet it felt like only moments before that they had been standing at the tree, watching it burn while the crazed denizens of Helsbridge hacked and battered her best friend.

Her *only* friend.

Rab could die for all she cared. *He* had done this. *He* had brought death and destruction, not just to Sammo, but to the whole town. Rab Macleod deserved nothing but an eternity of violent suffering.

"Lucy, hurry!" Her father urged her onwards. "Come on!" He grabbed her hand and dragged her past the scarecrows. There they were; the policeman with his whistle, the sunbathing couple in the striped swimwear, the angry butcher waving his fist, and the poor old lumberjack, forever chopping that same block of wood. They may have frightened off the few monsters that dared venture out this far, but Lucy sensed the time of the scarecrows was over. Now that the—

"Oof!"

A whatthefuck lurched out of nowhere, colliding with her father. It stood bestride him, the pincers clawing and tearing at his flailing arms. He managed to get his knees up, keeping the beast at bay even as it clamped a fiendish claw onto his forearm. Blood bubbled and squirted, and he screamed in agony.

Lucy glanced around in desperation. He may have betrayed her, but he was still her father.

With manic eyes, she ran for the nearest scarecrow.

The lumberjack.

"Gimme that," she snarled, snatching the axe from his grip. It was heavy, and took two hands to wield, but she arced it overhead as she raced to her father, burying the fearsome blade in the monster's body. The bulbous pink sac inflated with a freakish scream. She wrenched the axe loose and stepped back for a better angle, but the creature abandoned her father and turned towards her, rising up on four of its legs.

Shit.

The weak spot was no longer visible.

She backed away. "Dad! Get the pink... *thing!*"

The monster pounced.

She swung the axe like a golf club, cleaving open the creature's underside, but it knocked her flat. A flood of green ooze leaked from the gash in its belly and spilled onto her face. It burned, her skin sizzling, steam rising from her cheek as the pincers thrust at her body and arms.

The whatthefuck bucked, and she heard her dad shout, "I got him, Luce!"

The monster threw itself backwards and smashed into the lumberjack, but her dad clung on, his hands fully inserted into the pink membrane. When the monster tried to scream, all it made was a parping sound like a deflating balloon.

"Leave my daughter alone!" he roared, as he yanked the revolting shrimp from the sac and hurled it at the barn. It hit the wall with a splat, as the whatthefuck skittered around on dying legs, before collapsing, lifeless, into the long grass.

"You okay?" he asked as he ran to her, his hand clamped shut over the bloody rent on his forearm.

She touched her face, and when she removed her hand, her cheek was still attached by long threads of skin that resembled melted cheese.

"It burns," she said.

"Wait." her dad said. "I got you." Grimacing in pain, he reached into his shirt pocket and produced a crisp white handkerchief. "Stay still," he said, and dabbed at her face, studiously wiping the acidic residue from her skin. Lucy cried from the pain, and her salty tears stung the raw, burnt skin. She smelt her own sizzling flesh, and watched as the handkerchief smoked in her dad's fingers. He tossed the rag aside and helped her to her feet.

"Are you okay?" he asked. "Can you run?"

She nodded, and with the dead monster melting on the grass, they jogged for the van. The residents' cars were still parked in a long line out front, blocking the track. Had anyone made it out alive?

She increased her pace.

Almost free.

Free of this dreadful place, and those wretched people. She ran past the house, not caring that her belongings were in there. Not even her CDs.

"One sec," her dad said. "The keys are in the hall."

She swerved from her path and followed him inside, trying not to think of the way the mob had bullied and beaten her in her own home. Her dad grabbed the car-keys from the empty fruit bowl by the door.

"Wait right here," he said.

"Where are you going?"

"Won't be long!"

He ran for the stairs, taking them three at a time. Should she follow? She caught a glimpse of herself in a glass cabinet. Half her face drooped, the muscle and veins exposed, and her eye was—

"Go!" her dad shouted, bounding down the steps clutching sheaves of paper and a picture frame under one arm. *"Now!"*

Her face could wait. She darted from the house and

threw herself into the van, her dad tossing the paper into the footrest and jamming the keys in the ignition.

The engine started first time.

"Ha!" he cried, and spun the wheel with his good arm, manoeuvring over the grass in a tight circle. He slowed, letting the van idle as he gazed out the window.

"What are you doing?" asked Lucy. "Why have you stopped?"

"Look at it," he said.

The entire forest blazed. As far and as wide as Lucy could see, the trees burned beneath hungry flames that caressed the sky and threatened the rising moon.

"My god," her dad said.

"I don't think so," whispered Lucy.

She gazed across the field. The fire appeared to be spreading towards them in lurching waves, zigzagging through the grass.

"Drive," she said.

Her dad rested his hands on the wheel. "Is that what I think—"

"*Drive,* dad."

He squinted at the onrushing flames.

"Dad, for fuck's sake, *fucking drive!*"

Ignoring his injured arm, he threw the car into first gear and slammed the pedal. The wheels spun in the mud, refusing to catch.

"What's going on?"

"Stuck," he grunted.

"So unstick us!"

"I'm fucking trying!"

Lucy wound down her window and looked out.

"Please hurry," she said, for it wasn't just fire spreading through the field.

It was the monsters themselves.

Ablaze, they burst from the inferno, scurrying across the grassy field and leaving trails of scorched earth in their wake.

They were coming... and they were heading straight for the van.

30

Lucy's dad gunned the engine.

The tyres kicked up a muddy rainbow, but the van refused to budge.

The flaming monsters drew closer.

"They're coming!" she shouted.

Her dad adjusted the stick, putting the van into reverse. It lurched backwards, catching on loose earth, and he backed them up, spinning the steering wheel before jolting into first gear. The vehicle bumped over uneven terrain, heading for the track. The townsfolk's cars blocked the way, and deep pools of mud flanked the road on either side.

Lucy leaned out the window.

The monsters were almost upon them. The heat from their flaming bodies prickled her skin.

"Keep going!" she shouted.

Her dad slammed the pedal, and the van's right hand side mounted the track. The vehicle shuddered alongside a Land Rover, scraping the bulky machine's paintwork, then bashed a Volkswagen aside.

"Put your damn seatbelt on!" he roared, but Lucy was

too busy staring out the window in terror as the monsters bore down on them.

"Faster, dad, faster!"

They smacked into another 4x4, and Lucy came close to losing her balance. A hand grabbed the hem of her tee-shirt and yanked her back into the passenger seat, as they collided with a Fiat, the tyres skidding. He accelerated, pinballing off each subsequent vehicle. Something heavy thudded onto the van, and the steering wheel jerked out of her dad's hands. He was pale, and sweating, his left arm soaked in blood.

Lucy looked up, and touched her hand to the roof.

It was burning.

She shared a glance with her dad, then a pincered arm shattered the driver's side window.

"Drive, drive!" shouted Lucy.

He ducked out of the way of the groping, fiery claw. "You're not helping!"

They zoomed past the last parked car, and, leaning to the side, he manoeuvred the van fully onto the track without easing up on the gas. The monster on the roof shrieked as her dad took a tight bend at full speed, the low-hanging branches whacking at the doors and windshield. Two wheels left the ground, the van coming perilously close to tipping.

It was enough.

The monster lost its grip and smacked into the dirt. Her dad spun the wheel, quickly course-correcting and leaving the creature scrambling by the side of the road.

"Got you!" he shouted, and laughed maniacally. "Fucking got you, you bastard!"

"Keep your eyes on the road," said Lucy.

It was too soon to celebrate.

For as they screeched around another hairpin bend, and sped on until the track joined the main road, she knew they were not out of danger yet.

They still had to pass through Helsbridge.

The forest blazed alongside them as they drove, clouds of black smoke obscuring the road. Her dad switched on the full beams, but even they struggled to penetrate the miasma, as if the legends were true, and hell itself had crossed over into the everyday realm.

Lucy wound her window up and peered through the smouldering fumes. She saw no movement, save for spectral flames that devoured the trees and sent them crashing to the ground.

Neither Lucy nor her dad spoke. Words were insufficient to describe the nightmare taking place around them.

The headlights picked out a tall, unearthly shape in the black smog.

The war memorial.

They took the turn into Helsbridge, and for the first time, Lucy wondered what battle the memorial commemorated. A world war? Or a different conflict, one fought closer to home...?

She'd never know.

For as the wind changed direction, clearing the smoke, she knew she'd never return.

Carnage had descended on Helsbridge.

The buildings were aflame, and savaged bodies littered the road, the monsters fighting over the scraps. Isolated screams pierced the night as her dad deftly navigated past hollowed-out, burning cars. There were too many corpses to avoid, so he drove over them, the van juddering as they did so, and with each bump — as on the day of their arrival — the broken TV in the back of the van slid from side-to-side through a sea of its own shattered glass.

"What the fuck is that..." her dad whispered, slowing the van to a crawl as a huge shape materialised from within the smoke. It stalked through the fields, far bigger than the other monsters, and a limp, humanoid creature dangled upside-down beneath it.

"Just keep driving," she said, averting her glazed eyes from this new horror. She stared at the ruined shops, with their smashed windows and blood-streaked white walls. An old lady lay in pieces in front of the post office, her severed hand still clutching her walking stick, while a baby stroller lay on its side, the mother—

Movement caught her eye in the hiking shop.

Lucy leaned closer, her nose pressing against the glass.

A small figure hopped through the broken window and ran for the van. His face and clothes were black with soot, but even without his glasses, Lucy recognised Rab Macleod.

He reached the passenger door and placed bloodied hands on her window.

"Help me," he sobbed, pounding on the glass. "Let me in!"

A tear rolled down Lucy's cheek.

Everything around them — the burning forest, the decimated buildings, the torn and half-eaten corpses — was his fault. Or was it hers for trusting him?

"Lucy, please! You have to let me in!"

She pressed the lock down with her thumb.

"Drive on," she said to her dad without looking. He didn't question her.

"Wait!" shrieked Rab. "Where are you going? *Don't leave me here!*"

Her dad revved the engine, and off they drove. In the wing-mirror, Rab's silhouette faded into the smoke. She watched the flames from the approaching monsters light him up, and when he dropped to his knees, begging for mercy, she turned away.

You are now leaving Helsbridge, read a weathered white sign.

"Thank fuck for that," whispered Lucy. Her burns itched, and she scratched at the exposed, wet tissue. Ahead, the road curved into the darkness of the countryside.

"What now?" her dad asked.

Lucy was numb. The lights of a nearby town flickered in the distance.

"Just drive," she said.

"Where to?"

She stared at the distant mountains, and as the first of the evening's raindrops pattered erratically against the window, she clicked her seatbelt into the buckle and closed her eyes.

"Just... *drive.*"

PART IV

28 YEARS LATER

31

Dearest Lucy,
I'm dying.

Beneath the sterile glare of the hospital lights, Lucy
Brannigan re-read the note for the final time.

Twenty-eight years.

Where had it all gone?

Twenty-eight long years since she had last seen or
spoken to her father. He had been forty-four, then.

The age she was now.

Funny how quickly time passed. The older she got, the
more it seemed to speed up, until one day Lucy had looked
in the mirror and found a stranger peering curiously back at
her. But what about her father? Would he look the same? He
was seventy-two now. Not old, in the grand scheme of
things.

But old enough to die.

Everyone's old enough to die, she thought. *That's the great
tragedy of life.*

He was sick, the nurse had said. Every part of him. There was nothing they could do, she added, other than try to ensure he went comfortably.

He wasn't in pain. Not physically, anyway. The pills saw to that, while the machines kept him alive long enough for Lucy to catch the flight from Berlin to Edinburgh and reach the hospital.

Twenty-eight years.

How was it possible? She remembered the Helsbridge massacre like it happened last week. How could she forget, when her acid-scarred face and useless eye were there to remind her every day?

After that dark day, she and her father had driven aimlessly for months, sleeping in the van and rarely stopping anywhere for more than a couple of days. There was no insurance payout to draw on. They lost everything, except for the van, the clothes they wore, and her father's fucking manuscript.

She wondered if he'd ever finished it.

"He's ready for you," the nurse said.

Lucy nodded. She crumpled the note and dropped it into the bin. The hospital's claustrophobic walls were closing in on her, and she longed for fresh air, for the calming whisper of a gentle breeze.

But she could put it off no longer.

Steeling herself, she took a breath and opened the door to the private room, where a frail old man lay motionless in a bed. "Hi, dad," she said, and immediately the tears came. She hadn't said those words in so long.

The old man's head creaked towards her. *"You came."*

She wouldn't have recognised him.

He still had all his hair, though now it was snow white, but the rest of him...

"Looking good, huh?" he said. She struggled to hear him over the beeps from the monitors. "Please... sit."

He resembled a skeleton, his thin skin stretched taut over angular bones, his eyes dark pools of purple bruising.

"I wasn't sure you'd come," he said. His voice, at least, remained the same, albeit more gravelly than before. "It's been a long time."

"I know." She took his bony hand in hers. "Dad, I'm—"

"Don't," he said. "Not yet. Save it for the drive."

She choked back a sob. "I think we've done enough driving for one lifetime."

"No. One more. Just you and me, like the old days."

He was delirious. The nurse had told her that might be the case.

"I know what you're thinking," he said. "But there's time. There's always time."

"Not anymore. So let me say what I have to say."

"No," he said, offering a glimpse of the old Brian Brannigan. "I told you, you can tell me on the drive, and don't argue with your dying old man."

She broke down. There were too many emotions for her to focus. Relief. Sadness. Misery. Confusion.

But most of all, regret.

"And where will we drive to?" she asked.

"You know where. I want to go back. One last time."

A shiver ran through her. "There's nothing there anymore."

"Have you been?"

"No," she said. "This is my first time in Scotland since I left. It's been, what..."

"Twenty-seven years, eleven months, and eight days," he smiled. "Give or take a day or so. They don't have calendars in here."

"You won't be allowed to leave, dad. They say these machines are the only things keeping you... going."

"Then sneak me out. Like in my book, *The Wicked Doctor*. You ever read that one?"

She shook her head.

"That's okay," he said. "It wasn't my best, but it sold well. Enough for me to buy a house. I got one with two bedrooms, in case..." He smiled. "Well, the past is the past. Let's go."

"Why, dad?" she asked. "Why do you want to go back?"

He squeezed her hand. His grip was feeble, but insistent. "Why? Because I never did finish that story."

32

AND SO — JUST LIKE IN *THE WICKED DOCTOR*, AS HER DAD kept telling her — Lucy unhooked her father from the machines and sat him in a wheelchair with his backpack on his lap. Then she walked him out of the hospital without anyone noticing.

It was surprisingly easy.

Once they reached her car, she strapped his frail body into the passenger seat, folded the wheelchair, and placed it in the trunk. He clung to his backpack like it was his life-support machine.

She started the car. "You remember how to get there?"

"I'll never forget," he said. "Go north. I'll keep you right."

She looked at him, wrapped in a blanket and hugging his backpack, and wondered if he would make it all the way.

As they drove, they talked of the previous three decades. She told him of her life in Europe, moving from country to country, and of her battles with alcohol and drug addiction.

"Are you better now?" he asked. She liked when he spoke. It let her know he was still alive.

"I am," she said. "Mostly. It's been a long road. I met someone who helped me."

"I'm glad."

"What about you? You seem to be doing okay. I saw one of your books in the airport. I bought it."

"Which one?"

"Scandal in Scarlet. It looked a bit racy."

"Ha! That's a good one," he laughed. "Take the next turnoff, by the way."

"I remember," she said, surprised that she did.

Time had been unkind to Helsbridge. The surrounding trees had grown old, the branches hanging low as Lucy drove into the desolate remains of the town they had briefly called home. The buildings themselves were hollow shells, gutted by the fire, but nature had returned, and swamped the scorched edifices with vines and plants that grew from between cracked bricks.

"There's the cafe," said Lucy. "Remember we got cakes from there after we went shopping?"

"Was that the night you made dinner for me and Elli?"

"Yeah," she smiled. "Your first date."

"Our penultimate date."

She pulled up alongside the war memorial, the only thing that seemed to have survived intact. "This is where I got the bus to school."

"You said you didn't want me to drop you off."

"Dad, that van... can you blame me?"

"That van saved our lives," he said. "I still have it. I guess, soon, it'll be yours, if you want it."

"Is the TV still in the back?"

He laughed at that, then choked.

Lucy gripped the wheel. "Are you sure you want to do this?"

"I have to," he said. "And I think you do, too. We have to put all this behind us. You need to live your life unencumbered by the past... and I need to end mine the same." He put his hand on her knee. "It's time to go home."

They drove down the empty road until they came to the turnoff, and took the dirt track that led to the farmhouse. The abandoned cars and rusted SUVs were still there, the tyres flat, the windows broken. They passed them without a thought, for their gaze was focused solely on the building.

It still stood, as did — somehow — the scarecrows. Well, some of them, anyway. It was hard to tell, as the wild grass had grown so tall it obscured most of the figures.

She parked in the shadow of the farmhouse. "I never thought I'd see this place again."

"I always knew we'd come back. One day."

"Wanna go in?"

"No. But you go. I'll save myself for the next part."

"Okay," she said. "I'd like to see my room again. I'll just be a moment." She didn't want to leave him alone for too long. Did he really think he'd have the strength to go all the way? The chair wouldn't make it, and she doubted she could carry him. She wondered if the nurses had noticed he was missing yet.

The front door was unlocked, and she entered.

Apart from the weeds that sprouted from the floorboards, and the thick layer of animal droppings, it was as they had left it. In her room, tattered posters hung from the wall, her CDs neatly stacked in their tower. She picked up *Siamese Dream,* the booklet damp with rot, and slotted it into place. The torn poster of Brandon Lee watched over her as she stood by the window.

The forest was long dead, and yet, amongst the acres of burnt woodland, a single tree thrived. It towered over the rest, and upon its regal branches grew leaves as rich and golden as the afternoon sun.

His home.

She ran down the stairs and out the front door. Her father waited in the long grass by the crispy remains of the butcher scarecrow.

"Thought I'd get a head start," he said.

She walked to him. He hadn't gotten far. "You're incorrigible, *Brian.*"

"I always hated when you called me that."

"And *I* hated when you called me Luce."

He chuckled, and took her hand. "Did you see it?"

"See what?"

"You know what I mean." His eyes sparkled. "A while back, I saw it in a dream." He took a fragile breath. "And that's why I knew we had to come."

She let the words sink in. "It's there. I saw it."

"And how does it look?"

"It's beautiful. Just like I remember."

"Then why are we standing around gassing?" he asked. "Take my backpack, would you? It's not long now."

"I know," she said, placing the pack over her shoulders and taking his arm. "Not long now."

∼

The walk was laborious, but eventually, they made it to the tree with the golden leaves.

Father and daughter, one last time.

It was getting late, so Lucy sat her dad on a fallen log and prepared a fire. Not wishing to set the entire forest ablaze again, she cleared the area and surrounded the small campfire with stones. Then she sat by her father's side and watched the flames flicker.

"You smoke?" he asked, as she lit a cigarette.

"Yeah, but don't start. I swapped heroin for nicotine. It's a fair trade."

"I was only going to ask for one. It's been a while."

She passed him her lit cigarette and sparked up another. The fire warmed them, and the soft, yellow glow took years off her dad.

"I know you blamed me," he said.

She sat in silence, watching the fire.

"I was only looking out for you. You're my *daughter*. I would have given my own life to keep you safe." He took a draw on the cigarette, and coughed. "I know he was your friend, and that you loved him. And for what it's worth, I'm sorry."

Lucy stared at the tree. It still bore the scratches from Sammo's claws. "I'm sorry, too. I gave you such a hard time."

"You were a kid."

"That doesn't matter. You worked hard to give me a good life. And then my stubbornness got Miss Wade killed, and I think that's what hurt the most. That, thanks to me, you lost your last chance at happiness."

The fire crackled.

"It wasn't my last chance," he said, and put a shaky arm around her. "It just took a while to get another one. Twenty-seven years, eleven months, and eight days."

"Give or take a day or so," she said.

The sun was setting, the campfire holding off the encroaching darkness.

Her dad gestured towards his backpack. "Pass me that, would you?"

"What the hell you got in here, anyway?"

He laughed, and tried to open the pack, his wasted hands fumbling with the zipper. "Goddam it," he muttered, the cigarette clenched between his teeth. She offered to help, but he managed, and removed a thick wad of paper from inside. The corners of the sheets blew in the wind as he handed them to her.

"Is that..."

"My manuscript. I never did finish it."

She stared at the reams of paper, memories flooding over her. There must have been hundreds of pages. "Why have you..."

She looked at the fire, burning brightly, and understood his intentions.

"Dad, no. You risked everything for this. You were a real idiot."

"It wasn't just my manuscript. I had to get that photo of your mum."

"But... how long have you been working on this?"

"Most of my life, it feels." He smiled wryly. "I never could figure out how to end the damn thing."

"There's still time," she said, though they both knew that wasn't true.

"Doesn't matter. After a while, I began to understand. It was never my story to tell." He held her close, and she started to cry. "It was always yours."

He laid his hand across the pages.

"Do it, Lucy. Burn it, and let's say goodbye to the past forever."

She held the bundle in her hands. Her father's life's work. The idea that had revitalised him, that made him dream again. She couldn't...

"Please," he said, his voice as fragile as porcelain.

Clutching the manuscript, she walked towards the fire and knelt, reverentially laying the pages in the ravenous flames. The edges burned brown, the words vanishing in a fiery vortex. She stepped back, the wind catching tiny fragments of the document and spiralling them through the air. She took a seat next to her father and watched his face. He was crying. She reached into her jacket and removed a crisp white handkerchief.

"Here," she said. "Use this."

He took it, laughed, and dabbed at his eyes. "I wonder what... great man... taught you to carry one of these."

"We'll never know," she smiled.

"I'm glad... we got to spend... one more day together." The words no longer came easily to his lips. "Dying... doesn't seem so bad... if it's by your side."

"You never could do things normally, could you?"

She knew what he was going to say.

"Normal... is overrated."

"I know, dad. I know it is."

He tried to hand her the handkerchief. She waved him away. "Keep it. You might need it."

He didn't answer.

"I love you, dad," she said, and kissed his head. He was so cold.

She looked down at his limp hand. The handkerchief trembled in the wind.

"Let's just sit awhile and watch the fire," she said. "You and me, one last time."

And as they sat on the fallen tree, one propping the other up, Lucy listened to the heavy footsteps in the undergrowth, and the familiar, comforting grunt as an old friend lumbered along the trail. She felt his breath on her neck, and when he sat beside her, she took his soft paw in her hand.

The wind howled, igniting the campfire and sending the last scraps of paper billowing across the forest.

Tears rolled down Lucy's cheeks, yet still she smiled.

For after decades of searching — twenty-seven years, eleven months, and eight days, give or take a day or so — the story of the little girl who befriended a monster had finally found the perfect ending.

And her dad would have been so damn proud.

AFTERWORD

I hope you enjoyed Summer of the Monsters. This is my first book since leaving my day job of twenty-four years and going full-time as a writer, and I'm only able to do so because of readers like you who support truly independent authors.

So, thank you! It means the world to me.

The idea for this one had been percolating for a while, and I wrote the first draft in a manic burst after quitting my job. It was written concurrently with my next book, the ultra-extreme gore-fest Death Spell, and for a while I considered publishing both on the same day purely because they are so dissimilar.

After having a chat with my Patreons about it, I decided to space them out a little, because let's face it, one would inevitably get lost in the shuffle, but I still like the idea of releasing two wildly opposite books together, kinda like when all four members of KISS put out solo albums on the same day back in 1978. (For the record, Paul Stanley's album was the best of the four, and Peter Criss's isn't as bad as you've heard.)

Anyway, back to the book. There are quite a few locations featured in the story that are based on real places from my own childhood. The town of Helsbridge is actually the lovely little Scottish village Carrbridge, due to the presence of an 18th Century packhorse bridge, a holdover from an earlier draft that featured Lucy crossing a literal bridge to hell in the woods. Carrbridge is much nicer than Helsbridge though, and also has a really fun outdoor adventure park called Landmark that makes for a great family day out.

The war memorial is a pretty common sight in small towns and villages, but this particular one was based on the cenotaph in Boat of Garten, which is situated about thirty minutes walk from the key inspiration for the book, a place called The Yard.

The Yard is a small, isolated cottage nestled in the woods that for many years was surrounded by bizarre scarecrows and life-size figurines. We used to visit every year on our Highland holidays, and there was always some weird new thing to gawp at. A generator chugged endlessly from a shed beside the building, and there were wrecked cars dotted around, so it always reminded me of The Texas Chain Saw Massacre.

Sadly, all the figures from the garden are long gone. The cottage remains, though. I was there this summer, and that generator was still going strong. The weird thing is, in the thirty-or-so years we've been visiting, I've never once seen a human being there.

~

As always, thanks to my wonderful wife Heather for her support in my decision to write full time, and to Boris the pug for keeping me company.

A hearty thanks to my parents for taking my brother and I to the Highlands every year, a tradition I maintain to this day.

Cheers to Mark Bell for his amazing cover illustration. A pleasure to work with you, buddy!

Shoutouts to Steve Stred and Connor Corbett for being two kool dudez.

Two thumbs up to Carl John Lee for managing to keep a secret for almost five years.

And once more, because I can never say it enough, thanks to you, reader. You're fucking awesome, and your hair is nice, and everyone secretly fancies you.

Carrbridge — from left-to-right, that's my dad, my brother, and me.

The only photo I have of The Yard where you can see one of the figures.

MUSIC

For this book, I listened to a whole host of diverse music during the writing process, including — inevitably — a lot of 90s alt-rock/grunge. For the bulk of the book, though, I mostly used the following albums and movie soundtracks:

The Resurrected — Charles Band
Twin Peaks: Season Two — Angelo Badalamenti
My Neighbour Totoro — Joe Hisaishi
The Boy and the Heron — Joe Hisaishi
Spirited Away — Joe Hisaishi
Howl's Moving Castle — Joe Hisaishi
Gentle Breeze — PIPER
Sunshine Kiz — PIPER
Summer Breeze — PIPER

ACKNOWLEDGMENTS

Special Thanks to my Patreons —
    Adam Soll
    Anna the Cheddar Goblin
    Audie Schultz
    Brendan Fitz
    Courtney Pearson
    Danielle Chiarappa Perkowitz
    Destinie
    Elli Wade
    Isaiah Woodyard
    Jason Zuriff
    Joctan Hernandez
    Josh Heaps
    Joshua Carter
    Kala Vining
    Matt McCleland
    Mel Kaye
    Meredith Jensen
    Miss Kitty Fantastico
    Nicola Swordy
    Nicole Stephens
    Noah Andruss
    Peter Jilmstad
    Rebecca Vale
    Rob Jeromson
    Rochelle Hennings

Ryan Orgel
Sarah Brown
Steve Stred
Tyler Geis
Vickie Allan

ALSO BY DAVID SODERGREN

The Forgotten Island

Night Shoot

Dead Girl Blues

Maggie's Grave

The Navajo Nightmare (with Steve Stred)

The Perfect Victim

Satan's Burnouts Must Die!

The Haar

And By God's Hand You Shall Die

Rotten Tommy

Writing as Carl John Lee

The Blood Beast Mutations

Horror House of Perversion

Cannibal Vengeance

Horror House of Perversion 2: The Slaughtered Lambs

Psychic Teenage Bloodbath

Death Freaks on Hell's Highway

Psychic Teenage Bloodbath II